CIRCUS DAN

CIRCUS DAN

By

GEORGE MORSE

Author of
Extra!

THE GOLDSMITH PUBLISHING CO.
CHICAGO

CONTENTS

CIRCUS DAN

CIRCUS DAN

Chapter I

THE BIG ACT

Dan Tierney stopped beside the desk of the city editor of the Ralston Review.

"Have you got any extra passes for the Majestic tonight?" the star feature writer asked.

"Here's a couple for the first row balcony," replied Eddie Jackson, shoving a pair of blue pasteboards toward Dan. "I didn't know you were a vaudeville fan."

"I'm not as a rule," grinned Dan, "but I always enjoy a circus act and I've heard this week's bill at the Majestic is unusually good."

"You're welcome to all that kind of entertainment you want, no elephants and giraffes for yours truly," said Jackson, turning back to the pile of copy he was preparing for the next day's editions of the Review.

Farther down the long editorial office Fred Watkins, the assistant sports editor, was still at his desk. The top was littered with papers but Dan cleared a space and draped his long legs over a corner of the desk.

"I am," said Fred tartly, "slightly busy. In fact, I'm very busy writing a long story on the championship prospects of the basketball teams in the city league."

Dan waved the blue pasteboards before Fred's eyes.

"Regardless of your present rush," he suggested, "how about going to the Majestic to-night?"

"Passes?" inquired Fred suspiciously.

"Two. First row in the balcony."

"Then count me in. If I don't like the show I can sleep. Where do we meet?"

"Better make it in front of the theater at seven-thirty. I've got to chase out and get a story about a fellow who's been making a hobby of building miniature locomotives."

"That's no hardship for you," jeered Fred. "You spend all of your extra time down in the railroad yards anyway."

Dan went downstairs where he signed the register for one of the Review's cars. Going back to the garage at the rear of the building he took a low, fast roadster and guided it out into the stream of late afternoon traffic.

It was early January and with a thin drizzle hanging over the city, street lights had been turned on early. His destination was far on the other side of the great, sprawling mid-western metropolis and it was well after five o'clock when Dan arrived.

The builder of miniature locomotives, only a little older than the star feature writer, was a mechanical wizard and the minutes slipped away unnoticed as Dan watched small-sized Atlantic and Pacific type flyers perform on the track. It was after six o'clock when he started back down town with a sheaf of notes comprehensive enough for a column and a half story.

Dan stopped at a convenient restaurant, ordered his dinner, and scanned the notes. There was something about railroading that had always appealed to him. He could see adventure riding in the cab of every train as it pulled out of the down town terminal and he often thought that he would have made a better railroad man than reporter. But in that respect the city editor of the *Review* would have differed with him for Dan was singularly well fitted as a newspaper man. In the first place he was unusually level-headed when news was breaking hot and fast and he had the faculty of writing his stories simply yet with sweeping power. Any story from Dan's typewriter fairly sparkled with good writing. On top of all that he was physically capable of standing the strain of daily newspaper work.

Dan stood a little over six feet. His shoulders were broad and his hands large and capable. His hair and eyes were brown. He usually weighed around 175 pounds and three years of varsity football in high school when he had made the all-city team the last two years had endowed him with the ability to take care of himself under almost any circumstance.

When Dan had finished his dinner and returned down town, it was time to meet Fred. He parked the Review's car near the theater for he would go to the office later and write the story of the builder of miniature locomotives.

One thing about Fred, thought Dan as the assistant sports editor hurried up, he was always on time. Dan presented the passes and they soon found themselves in the front row of the balcony. The motion picture on the program finished as they sat down.

"We got here just right," said Fred. "It was a wild animal picture and most of that kind of stuff is faked."

"There's going to be a stage act tonight that isn't faked," Dan said. "The headliner on the bill is Capt. Bob McMasters with his lion and tiger act."

"Probably a bunch of feeble old lions and toothless tigers," scoffed Fred.

"There's nothing feeble about the animals or the act. I saw it with the Great United last year when the show started out of winter quarters. Believe me, it's a real thriller and it will be especially so tonight for McMasters won't have as large an arena as he uses with the circus."

"I still think the animals are too old to fight," insisted Fred.

The orchestra completed the overture and a quartet of jugglers flashed into action. The entire bill was devoted to circus acts with a ringmaster announcing the succeeding events on the program. It was smooth, fast entertainment with lively clowns, daring aerialists and marvelously supple tumblers.

"Now that's what I like," said Fred as an

acrobat swung far out over the audience on his trapeze.

"I suppose you're hoping he'll fall into the audience."

"I'm not quite that heartless."

While two clowns amused with a burlesque of a boxing match, the scene was being set back stage for the headliner of the evening. Above the cries of the clowns and the answering applause from the audience, the roars of the lions were plainly audible.

"Kind of gives a fellow the shivers, at that," said Fred.

"Oh, you don't need to worry," Dan retorted. "Of course they're 'feeble old lions and toothless tigers.'"

The clowns disappeared, the house lights darkened, and the curtain shot up. A spotlight disclosed the trim figure of the famous young animal trainer, Capt. Bob McMasters, standing beside the huge steel arena. Then the full lights flashed on, revealing the cage filled with milling beasts.

"My gosh, is he going in there?" asked Fred, grabbing the arms of his seat and leaning forward intently.

With a chair in one hand, whip in the other and a holstered gun at his side, the young trainer stepped into the cage. A lion sprang toward him but the sharp crack of the whip sent the beast lunging to one side. Captain Mc-Masters worked slowly, always careful to see that his back was never left exposed to the vicious lash of a huge paw. The lions appeared more tractable than the tigers, who fought every step of the way as he drove them back to their places.

It was a daring, breath-taking exhibition of nerve and skill. Dan was fascinated by the trainer's coolness. Only once had he been forced to fire a blank into the face of one of the tigers. Slowly the pyramid of animals was being built against the back wall of the arena.

Dan was watching one magnificent beast. The lion had caused no trouble when Captain McMasters drove it to its stool but since taking its place had watched every movement of the trainer.

"How old do you think McMasters can be?" asked Fred.

"Not a whole lot older than we are. About 24 or 25, I suppose."

"Seeing this circus act reminds me that Hugh Adams, owner and general manager of the Great United, was in the office late this afternoon with Mr. Benbow."

"They've been close friends for a number of years," said Dan recalling that Frank Benbow, owner of the Review, always planned to pass a part of his summer vacation with the Great United when it was on tour.

"Mr. Benbow sent out word he wanted to see you and when Jackson told him you were out on an assignment, he left a note for you to see him the first thing in the morning."

"Wonder if the Review is going to put me on the list of unemployed?"

"That's one thing you don't have to worry about," smiled Fred. "Jackson would fire half of the staff before he'd let you go."

Dan grabbed Fred's arm hard.

"Watch the second lion from the right in the first row," he whispered. "That big fellow hasn't any love for his trainer."

"He's quiet enough."

"I know, but he never takes his eyes off Mc-Masters. See how tense his muscles are?"

"You're right. He's like a spring ready to let go."

The young trainer was having trouble with a stubborn tigress on the left side of the cage. The tawny animal was rushing back and forth, lashing at him with her paws, and he was finally compelled to fire a blank at her before she decided to leap onto her stool. The act was nearing its climax. There was only one more lion to get into place and McMasters backed slowly across the ring.

Dan and Fred, watching the second lion from the right, saw the animal shift its weight slightly. In the flash of a second the trainer's back was uncovered as he turned toward the one beast which was running back and forth. The lion gathered itself for the lunge. Fred broke suddenly under the tension and gave vent to his feelings in a piercing cry that rang through the theater.

At the same moment the lion leaped. Something in Fred's sudden cry warned McMasters of the attack and without turning to see what was the matter, he dropped to the floor. The lion twisted wildly, but the impetus of his leap carried him over the trainer. Before he could turn and plunge back, McMasters had regained his feet and backed toward the door through which he could escape if necessary.

"He'd better get out of there," Fred mumbled to Dan. "Gosh, I feel cheap after yelling like that. Everybody in the balcony is looking my way."

"None of the rest of us had the sense or wits to yell," replied Dan. "Your cry may have saved McMasters' life."

The near accident failed to daunt the trainer and the act went on until he had every lion and tiger in its place with 23 of the jungle brutes ranged along the curving back wall of the cage. Stepping out of the steel arena carefully, he bowed as the audience thundered its applause.

"He looks like a real fellow," observed Fred, as the curtain finally fell.

"One thing, he's got an abundance of nerve. Think of going into that den of animals twice a day when the circus is on tour."

They remained to view the news reel and as they prepared to leave when the feature started an usher appeared beside Fred.

"Are you the gentleman who yelled a warning to Captain McMasters during his act?" he inquired.

"Guilty."

"Captain McMasters would like to see you in

his dressing room if you can spare the time," said the usher.

"Go ahead," urged Dan. "I'll trail along. It will make a good feature story. Think of the headline: 'Lusty Lungs of Sports Editor Saves Life of Famous Wild Animal Trainer.'"

"You write me into a feature story and I'll punch your nose," promised Fred, but there was no hint of actual violence in his voice and in view of the fact that he stood a bare five feet six and had a hard time balancing the scales at 120 pounds, Dan was safe.

Following the usher, they went down to the main floor and were led backstage, where stagehands were busy tearing down the large arena. The dressing rooms were in the basement and they went down a ramp.

"Captain McMasters' room is No. 3," said the usher. "Just knock on the door. He's expecting you."

A pleasant voice invited them to enter and they stepped inside to be greeted by the famous animal trainer. Bob McMasters swung around from his make-up table to face them. A towel was draped around his shoulders but he had finished removing his make-up.

"I'm Bob McMasters of the Great United circus," he said. "Please sit down."

"I'm Dan Tierney and this is Fred Watkins. We're both on the staff of the Review," said Dan.

"Mighty glad to know you," smiled Bob, who at close range appeared to be almost the same age of the newspapermen. "Which one of you warned me that old Jup was on the war-path?"

Fred smiled rather sheepishly.

"I was so excited I couldn't help yelling," he confessed.

"If you hadn't I would have been on my way to a hospital," said Bob McMasters. "That's the trouble with a lion. You never know just when he's going to go bad on you. As a rule Jup is one of my best performers. Oh, he roars a little about getting up on the pedestal but he never means it."

"Do you have many close calls like the one tonight?" asked Dan, who saw an opportunity to get a feature story.

"Not many, or I wouldn't be putting them through their paces twice a day. I've been clawed badly several times."

Dan noticed several scars on the trainer's right forearm and he pursued his questions.

"Are you on a long vaudeville tour?"

"I'm just finishing up a six weeks' swing around the Elite circuit in the middle west. This is the last stand and I'm taking the outfit back to the winter quarters of the circus."

"It doesn't seem to me your act is as large as the one you had in the Great United last spring," said Dan.

"I can't work as many animals in the smaller arena on the stage," explained Bob. "As soon as I'm settled in winter quarters I'm going to work out some new stunts for the act next spring. I used 28 animals in the arena last year and I hope to add about seven more. That will give me the largest wild animal act of its kind in the world."

"It ought to be a good drawing card for the circus," suggested Dan.

"I hope so. Business was poor last season and we came in off the road early."

The trainer glanced at his watch.

"I've got to go," he said. "The trucks with the act will be leaving for winter quarters in a few minutes. Believe me, I'm grateful that you fellows were in the audience. Most people would think Jup's leap just a part of the act and that would have been too bad for me. Be sure to look me up when the Great United opens the season here this spring."

"We'll do that," promised Fred.

As they emerged from the theater, the blast of an ambulance siren greeted their ears and a long, blue machine raced by. Normally they would have thought little of the incident but from the street to their right came the sound of another ambulance. Bells and sirens were going on every side.

"Come on," cried Dan. "There's news breaking somewhere!"

Chapter II

RACING FOR NEWS

The two young newspapermen piled into the staff car. Dan switched on the ignition, tramped on the starter, and the motor responded with a roar. Ignoring traffic rules, he swung the machine around in the middle of the block. The sound of the ambulance's siren had died to a faint wail as they set out in full pursuit.

Stop lights favored them and they shot down the boulevard at a hair raising pace.

"You're doing better than fifty," warned Fred. "We'll get picked up sure for speeding."

"Can't help it. Hear those sirens? Every ambulance and police car in town is on its way out southwest. Something big has happened."

"The stop light's going against us!" cried Fred.

Dan jammed on the brakes. The tires slid smoking along the pavement but they stopped before skidding into the intersection. A traffic officer who had glimpsed their wild approach hurried toward them.

"What's the idea making a race track out of this boulevard?" he demanded. "Can't you read those forty mile an hour signs?"

"Sorry, officer," said Dan respectfully. "We're from the Review and we're trying to catch up with the ambulance up ahead. What's happened?"

Dan produced his reporter's badge and the officer appeared satisfied.

"Train wreck about fifteen miles out on the Central Western," he replied. "Passenger and a freight hit head-on."

"Have you heard just where it happened?" Dan asked quickly.

"About two miles east of Peters station."

The lights flashed to "go" and with a hasty "thanks, officer," Dan let out the clutch and the long, low roadster shot ahead, weaving its way through the traffic.

The scream of a siren forced them over to the side of the boulevard and as Dan slowed the car Fred looked back to see what was coming.

"It's a salvage crew from the fire depart-

ment," he cried. "They're running past everything."

"Here's where we get out of town in a
hurry," said Dan grimly. "Hang on."

The red salvage wagon, its siren clearing the
way, roared past and on the echo of its exhaust
Dan shot after it. The roadster gained speed
rapidly and within two blocks was directly behind the salvage outfit. Through stop lights
they sped and traffic scattered before the stri-
dent warning from the fire department car.

Looking far ahead, Dan saw that they were
past the last stop lights. He tramped on the
accelerator and the roadster shot past the salvage crew. Sixty, sixty-five and seventy miles
an hour said the speedometer. They over-
hauled an ambulance, loaded with internes and
nurses. Half a mile beyond they overtook two
more ambulances and a little further out of the
city raced by a police car.

"You keep on at this rate," Fred shouted in
Dan's ear, "and we'll be the first car to reach
the scene of the wreck."

"That's what I'm trying to do," replied Dan
between set lips. He was thankful that he had
chosen the roadster to drive that afternoon for

it was by far the fastest machine the Review owned.

"Hey, look who's ahead of us," cried Fred. "That brown car belongs to the Times."

"They won't be ahead very long. We're making speed."

The roadster lunged ahead with a new burst of speed and slowly but surely they pulled up on the machine carrying reporters from the other afternoon paper. As they roared by Dan caught a glimpse of Al Simmons at the wheel and he chuckled inwardly for Al was his rival feature writer on the Times and had been known to boast of his ability as a driver.

They were now ahead of all of the machines bound for the wreck and Dan was determined to keep them in the van.

"You know the country around Peters station?" asked Fred.

"Only in a general way. I've been out there on picnics several times. We leave the paving in a couple more miles and from then on it's a dirt road."

As they sped along the smooth ribbon of concrete, a daring plan evolved in Dan's mind. He decided it was worth the chance and as they neared a corner, jammed on the brakes and skidded the roadster onto a side road.

"There aren't any signs here that say this is the road to Peters station," protested Fred.

"You just hold onto your seat. I'm driving."

The road was extremely rough and thirty miles an hour was the fastest Dan dared to drive. For two miles they bounced over the ruts.

"I can see lights over to our right," cried Fred.

"That's the wreck then," replied Dan. "The railroad crossing is just ahead."

The roadster rolled up the incline to the crossing and Dan threw the car into low gear.

"Say, what's the idea?" cried the startled Fred as Dan swung the car along the right-of-way.

"You want to get there first, don't you?"

"Sure, but——."

"Then we're getting there first."

With two wheels straddling one of the rails, they sped along the right of way. Ahead of them lanterns were bobbing up and down and the glow of the fire in one of the wrecked locomotives reflected against the escaping steam cast a weird radiance over the whole scene.

"We're trapped!" shouted Fred as a small trestle loomed ahead. "There's a train coming around the curve behind."

Dan glanced over his shoulder. Half a mile back a headlight was visible rounding a curve. There was plenty of time for their own escape but the roadster would be smashed and he would have a hard time explaining the accident satisfactorily to even such a lenient city editor as Eddie Jackson.

Shifting the car into low again he started ahead.

"What are you going to do?" demanded Fred.

"Get across the bridge. Hop out now if you want to."

"I'll stick," said Fred as the car started bumping over the trestle. Fortunately it was a short span and the train was slowing down rapidly. Once on the other side they were safe for the ground was level and Dan drove the roadster off the right-of-way.

Leaping out of the car, they hurried ahead to ascertain the seriousness of the wreck. The

sign on the observation car of the limited was
still illuminated and Dan read the name of the
train.

"Gosh, it's the Southwestern limited, crack
train of the line," he whistled. "They've got
a fifty mile an hour schedule for the first 143
miles out of Ralston. They must have been
doing better than sixty right along here. It
must be some wreck up on the front end."

The back end of the train was deserted but
when they reached the head Pullman they
found an excited group of passengers.

"Anyone hurt?" called Dan.

"The engine crew of the freight is missing,"
replied someone.

"How about the passengers on the limited?"
Dan fired the question at a porter.

"No passengers hurt, boss, but the engine
crew is all stove in."

Reaching the head end, they surveyed the
scene in the meager light of the trainmen's lanterns and the ruddy glow from the open firebox
of the twisted freight engine, which had rolled
over on its side.

The passenger locomotive was in the ditch
and the first baggage car was astraddle the

rails. Beyond that there was a tangled heap of freight cars.

"Find out how many cars on the freight are piled up and see if you can talk to any members of the crew," Dan told Fred. "I'll see what I can learn from the trainmen on the limited."

The story of the wreck was not hard to secure. The operator at Peters station had failed to stop the freight and get it on a siding. As a result the trains had met head-on.

"Where's the crew of the freight engine?" Dan asked the conductor of the limited, displaying his reporter's badge when that official was inclined to ignore the question.

"I'm afraid they're under the engine," replied the trainman. "We haven't been able to find them and the steam from their engine is too hot for us to get down there. Guess we won't know until the big hook gets here and we can jerk the engine out of the ditch."

"Strange no one on the limited was seriously injured," said Dan.

"The fireman's got a sprained leg and the baggage man was knocked out by the shock, but the engine crew jumped just before they struck."

Dan secured the names of the missing engine crew of the freight and also of the trainmen aboard the limited. He would have to stop at Peters station to learn the name of the operator whose carelessness had been responsible for the accident.

The locomotive which had chased Dan and Fred across the trestle nosed into the back end of the limited and a short time later the cars which had remained on the rails were started back toward Ralston where they would be routed over another line.

The shrilling of a siren drew their attention and Dan saw the first of the ambulances coming across a pasture which bordered the right-of-way. Behind it was the brown sedan containing the Times' reporters.

"We got here a good fifteen minutes ahead of them," Dan chuckled.

"You mean we almost didn't get here," retorted Fred. "Every time I think of bouncing across the trestle with that locomotive thundering down behind us I get shaky."

"Yes, but think of all the first hand information we obtained by getting here first."

"I'd just as soon get the facts some other

way," grumbled Fred. "I still think my neck is worth something."

The wrecker from Ralston arrived a few minutes later and started the task of clearing the right-of-way. It would be morning before the freight engine was righted and Dan decided they might as well return to the city.

On the way back they stopped at Peters station and he ascertained the name of the telegraph operator whose neglect had sent the two trains crashing into each other.

They were halfway back to the city when a machine roared past them, bound in the direction of the wreck.

"See whose car it was?" asked Fred.

"Too busy keeping out of their way."

"It was Jack Mathews in one of the Review's cars. He may be sore when he learns you've got the whole story."

"I can't help that. Jack's on the night police assignment. He probably went to a show and didn't learn about the accident until it was over. At least he was trying hard to make up for lost time."

When they reached the city Dan checked the car in at the garage and they went up to the editorial office. A night editor who prepared the copy for the early edition the next morning was on duty.

"I hear there was quite a wreck tonight," he said.

"Two men probably killed and a couple of engines and a lot of freight cars smashed," said Dan.

"You been out there?" the night editor asked.

"We happened to hear the ambulances going out," explained Dan, "and we trailed along."

"You mean we led the parade," put in Fred. "No more rides like that for me."

"If you've got all of the facts, write a couple of columns tonight and I'll send it out for the early mail," said the night editor. "When Jack comes back he can put on a new lead if anything has developed since then."

"I'll get at it right away," promised Dan. "What are you going to do?" he asked Fred.

"I'm going home," replied the assistant sports editor, "and I only hope I don't dream about lions and trains. See you tomorrow."

Chapter III

THE STRANGE CALL

When Dan reached his own desk he found a note rolled into the top of his typewriter. Unfolding the slip he found that it was written in the cramped handwriting of the publisher of the Review.

"Please see me the first thing in the morning," read Dan.

He sat down at his desk and fingered the slip of paper. He wondered if the publisher was going to fire him. But he dismissed that thought shortly for all of the hiring and firing on the editorial staff was done by the city editor. Probably Mr. Benbow wanted a special feature story for the Sunday edition for on several occasions during the last year he had called upon Dan to write stories for him.

Dan rolled a sheet of copy paper in his machine and at the top of the page typed out the line, "DAN TIERNEY, TRAIN WRECK," which meant that the story was being written by Dan Tierney and that it concerned the train wreck. This was a guide to copy readers when stories were coming in thick and fast during the rush hours of the day and if there was some question they wanted to know about the story the line at the top gave them the name of the reporter and they could yell for him to come to the big copy desk which stood on a small, elevated platform at the far end of the room.

Dan wrote a graphic account of the train wreck, relating the failure of the telegraph operator to give the freight the proper orders and the head-on collision of the two trains outside Peters station. He went on to describe in detail the scene of the wreck and the wild race of the ambulances from the city through the countryside. When he leaned back from his typewriter and wrote "30" at the end of the story he found he had written nearly six pages of copy. The story would run a full two columns, perhaps a little more, for Dan used long sheets of copy paper. Oh, well, if the night editor thought it was too long Dan knew that individual would cut the story down with a few expert slashes here and there with his heavy black pencil.

The star feature writer scanned the pages carefully, correcting an error in spelling here and there or changing an adjective to make the story more powerful. Finally he was through and he picked up the sheets of copy and carried them to the copy desk.

On his way back to his own desk Dan glanced at the clock. It was almost midnight, far later than he had realized. He looked at the notes on his desk. He had two more stories to write, the features about the builder of miniature locomotives and Bob McMasters, the lion trainer. If he stayed at the office and wrote them it would be well after two o'clock before he reached home. The story about the locomotive builder was not scheduled until the Sunday edition, which gave him ample time to prepare it, and he knew he could write the one about the lion trainer the first thing in the morning.

"If that train wreck story is all right," Dan called to the night editor, "I'm going home."

"It's okay," replied the editor. "Mighty good yarn. Thanks a lot for coming in with it."

Dan said goodnight and hurried down the

two flights of stairs to the street. At the corner he caught a street car which took him within three blocks of his home. It was not until then that he actually realized how fatiguing the day had been. There had been plenty to do without racing out to Peters station after the story of the wreck but he knew that he wouldn't have wanted to miss that. He raided the ice box in the kitchen and sat down to drink a glass of milk and clean up the scraps of a chicken carcass he discovered in the ice chest.

The soft padding of feet on the back stairs warned him of the approach of his father, who came down in his pajamas and bathrobe to learn the news of the night. There was a close bond of companionship between Dan and his father and they often passed an hour in the evening discussing current happenings.

"Where were the ambulances going?" asked Tierney, senior, as he sat down beside his son and proceeded to help with the task of getting all of the meat off the chicken.

Dan told the story of the wreck in detail and his father listened intently.

"Your mother was inclined to worry a little when you didn't phone about having a late assignment but when I heard all of the ambulances I knew there must have been a serious accident."

Dan mentioned that the publisher of the Review wanted to see him the first thing in the morning.

"I wouldn't worry about it," his father said. "You've been doing some splendid work for the Review, and I happen to know that if anything should happen there you could get a job on the Times."

"I don't think I would want to work on the Times," replied Dan. "They stoop to some mighty low tricks to obtain stories. I've got some pride in how I get mine."

"That's the right way to look at it," his father agreed. "I feel sure that the Review usually benefits by its policy of fairness although there are occasions when the Times' tricky methods result in their getting a big story first."

"Do you two know what time it is?" asked a voice from the head of the stairs.

Dan's father glanced guiltily at the clock.

"One o'clock son," he said. "We'd better get to bed."

"We'll be up right away, mother," called Dan. The chicken had been picked clean and he placed his empty milk glass in the sink. With his father leading the way, he went upstairs and to bed.

Reporters who had handled night assignments were not required to appear at the office until 9 o'clock, but Dan tried to make it a practice to be there promptly at eight regardless of his previous night's work. He met Jack Mathews on the way upstairs. Jack looked white and tired.

"You're just the fellow I've been looking for," said Jack. "How did you know I was sleeping in a movie instead of covering the central police station last night?"

"I didn't."

"Then why did you go out and cover the wreck?"

"Just plain curiosity," grinned Dan. "Fred and I had come out of the Majestic when the ambulances started out and we went along to see what had happened."

"I've been on the story the rest of the night. Just finished writing a new lead for your yarn."

"How about the crew of the freight?"

"They never knew what hit them," said Jack. "They were still in the cab of their engine when the wrecker picked it up this morning."

"Did you get any pictures?"

"I brought back a camera full. Would have had more but I ran out of flash bulbs. Anytime I can help you out on a story, just let me know. Believe me, I appreciate what you did last night."

The large editorial room of the Review was alive with activity when Dan entered.

The city editor was giving his staff orders for the day. Some of them were starting out on their regular beats while others were being given special assignments. In a room adjoining the main office a battery of electric printers chattered as they brought in the news of the day from state and nation.

Jackson summoned Dan to his desk.

"Your story on the wreck was a nice piece of writing," he said. "Jack told me how you helped him on it. Have you got the story about the miniature locomotives yet?"

"I haven't written it," replied Dan, "but I have all the notes." He also explained about the incident at the theater and the feature he planned to write about the young lion trainer.

"Write the lion story first," said Jackson. "It will make an unusually good feature and especially since Fred's cry saved McMasters from probably serious injury. Have we got a picture of Fred?"

"I don't think so. He'll kick like the dickens if I use his name in the story."

"Just tell him I told you to do it. Then if he wants to protest he can come to me," grinned Jackson. "Also tell him to go down to the studio and have a picture taken at once. I'll send a note to the head engraver that we must have the picture in time for the noon edition."

"Are you putting me in your lion trainer story?" Fred demanded when Dan told him he was to go to the studio at once and have his picture taken.

"Orders are orders."

"Then you'll have to look for someone else to go to shows with you," Fred flung at him as he started for the studio.

Dan put Mr. Benbow's note on his desk as a reminder to see the publisher as soon as he came and started writing the feature about Bob

McMasters and the near accident at the theater the night before. It was an easy story to write, the kind that Dan enjoyed, and the words flowed swiftly and smoothly. He finished it in little less than an hour and placed it on the city editor's desk just as the publisher arrived.

"Good morning, Dan," greeted Mr. Benbow.

"Good morning, sir," replied Dan. "I have the note saying you want to see me."

"I certainly do," smiled Mr. Benbow, "but I want to wait until my old friend Hugh Adams arrives. As soon as he comes I'll call you."

The publisher went into his private office and Dan returned to his desk. The impending interview puzzled him. He wondered what it could mean, for Hugh Adams was the owner of the Great United circus, which featured Capt. Bob McMasters and his lion act as the headline attraction of the big show.

Chapter IV

AT WINTER QUARTERS

While waiting for the owner of the Great United, Dan turned his attention to writing the feature story on the builder of the miniature locomotives. He was half way through when he saw Mr. Adams entering the office of the publisher. A minute later Mr. Benbow called to Dan.

"I'll finish the story on the miniature locomotives as soon as I'm through in Mr. Benbow's office," Dan told the city editor before entering the quarters of the publisher of the Review.

Mr. Benbow's office was a spacious room with large windows on the north side. The desk was broad and grouped around it were large, easy-cushioned chairs. In one of these sat the owner of the Great United, who rose as Dan came in.

"Dan," said the publisher, "I want you to know Hugh Adams. He's not only a close friend but is also owner of one of the finest circuses in the world."

47

"I've often heard of Mr. Adams," smiled Dan as they shook hands. "I've seen his show a number of times and I've always enjoyed it."

"I try to have the highest class circus in the world," said the veteran showman. "It isn't the largest but it is the cleanest."

"Size doesn't always make a good circus," put in the publisher, "and the same thing applies to newspapers. I prefer the ethics of some of the smaller dailies to those of their big brothers. Which isn't getting down to the point of this meeting."

Turning to Dan, he asked a question which astounded the feature writer.

"Are you satisfied with your position here?"

Dan flushed. "That's a pretty direct question," he countered. "If you mean, will I be satisfied to spend the rest of my life as a feature writer, the answer is, 'I won't.' But if you want to know whether I'm satisfied at the present time, the answer is 'yes.'"

"Would you consider making a change?" pressed Mr. Benbow.

"Not to any other newspaper in Ralston and it would have to be something unusual to make me think of leaving the Review."

"This happens to be unusual."

"Then I would be glad to consider it."

The publisher appeared relieved and he turned to his friend with a smile.

"All right, Hugh," he said. "The rest of it is up to you."

Dan looked at the owner of the Great United. Hugh Adams was in his middle fifties, a man of great vitality. His dark hair was only thinly streaked with grey. There was an alive, ruddy color to his cheeks, and a flash of determination in his brown eyes. Dan felt an instant glow of liking for the circus man.

"I'll begin my story by going back about five years," said Adams as he settled deeper into the large, upholstered chair. "At that time a man by the name of Barney Hutchinson had a fourth interest in my show. He served as general manager and was actively in charge of the circus while I passed most of my time looking after silver mines I own in Colorado. To my astonishment and disgust, I learned that Hutchinson was putting grafters on the circus and it was getting a bad name. I hurried back and we had a showdown. As a result I forced Hutchinson to sell his interest and I started out to clean up the circus. It wasn't an easy thing to do for my show was attracting enormous crowds that season and the grafters were making an easy living. I finally managed to get rid of most of them and then found that Hutchinson was my rival. He had taken the money obtained from his share of the Great United and bought an interest in the Amalgamated."

"I thought the Langdon estate owned the Amalgamated," said Dan.

"It does," said Adams. "No finer showmen ever lived than the Langdon brothers, but when the last one of them died there was no one left to carry on the show and Hutchinson stepped in. He is a good circus man in that he knows how to select acts that will draw the crowds. He made a great deal of money for the first three years but two years ago the public began to realize that whenever they attended a performance of the Amalgamated they were going to be cheated someplace, either in change for their tickets to the big tent, the sideshow or when they bought something to eat. Hutchinson assembled a great outfit of short change artists but when the crowds started falling off even they couldn't make money. As a result for the last two years he's been out to break me."

"What's the object of that?" Dan asked.

"There are two reasons. One is for revenge because I forced him out of the Great United and the other is that my circus is gaining in popularity while the Amalgamated is losing. He's done some mighty rotten tricks in the last two years, playing cities the same date we have, tearing down our posters, trying to get grafters into my show and all kinds of things like that. Fighting Hutchinson, coupled with the depression, placed my finances in a precarious situation. In other years I could go on with profits from my silver mines carrying the show, if needed, but silver mining doesn't pay at present. I can lick Hutchinson in the end, but it is mighty expensive business."

"That's just where I come in," said the publisher of the Review. "I'm still more or less of a kid even if it is necessary to put about 60 candles on my birthday cake. I've always wanted to have a hand in the show business and when Hugh told me of his troubles with fighting Hutchinson, I bought a part interest in the Great United."

"You own a share in the Great United?" asked Dan incredulously.

"He owns about 30 per cent," said Mr. Adams, "and it's his money that makes it possible for the Great United to carry on the fight against Hutchinson."

"How can Hutchinson go on?" asked Dan. "He must be losing money?"

"He has the resources of the Langdon estate to draw upon, but when the executors of that estate finally realize how Hutchinson has been spending their money, he'll be looking for another job. In the meantime, I have a fight on my hands every day the show is on the road."

"I've been making a few suggestions to Hugh about plans for the coming season," said the publisher. "He agrees with me in a number and as a result there are going to be some changes in the personnel of the Great United. A little while ago, Dan, you said it would take a mighty unusual offer to make you consider leaving the news."

"That's right, Mr. Benbow."

"I've got just such an offer. Will you consider the job as chief press agent for the Great United?"

Dan stared at the publisher. Chief press agent for the Great United! Why it seemed impossible.

"Are you really serious?" he asked.

"We're mighty serious, Dan," said the publisher. "The position of chief press agent is highly important and we must have someone in whom we can place absolute trust when it comes to loyalty to the show. We feel that you would stick with the job to the end. If the season should prove unusually disastrous and the show is forced to end its tour early, there would always be a job waiting for you on the Review."

"What happened to the press agent last year?"

"We found that he was getting checks from two sources," said Mr. Adams, "one from our show and the other signed by Barney Hutchinson. The entire press staff was fired and it will be up to you to build a new organization if you accept the job."

"What do you say, Dan?" asked the publisher, with more than a trace of anxiety in his voice.

"It sounds mighty interesting, but I question whether I am fitted for the job. I wouldn't want to go into it unless I had a feeling that I could make a success. All I've ever seen of a circus is from a seat in the big tent."

"The successful press agent relies on a pleasant personality and a knowledge of newspapermen and their ways," said the general manager of the Great United. "It seems to me you are amply endowed with ability when it comes to those essentials. You should be able to pick up all of the necessary information in winter quarters before the show goes out on the road."

"Don't give us your answer right now," said the publisher. "We'll get in my car and run out to winter quarters. After a tour of the place you should be able to make up your mind."

Dan readily assented to the suggestion and within the hour they were at the village of Coralville, just beyond the city limits, where the Great United made its winter quarters. Turning off the main road, their car passed under a wooden arch, on which were painted the words, "Winter Home of Great United Circus, the Highest Class Show in the World." A long lane led to the main buildings and in a pasture to the right Dan noticed a large herd of camels. Their coats were heavy and they appeared to be in fine condition.

"Do they stay out in the pasture all winter?" he asked Mr. Adams.

"They're out most of the time. Only in the very coldest weather do they come up to a shed for shelter."

They stopped before a rambling old brick house which served not only as the home for the general manager but as the main office for the circus.

"The office is the least interesting thing on the place," said Mr. Adams. "We'll visit the elephant barn first."

Crossing the large yard, they entered a huge barn, the lower floor of which was the home of the elephant herd while the haymow was used to store feed for the pachyderms.

"Just taking some friends through the barns," Mr. Adams called to the head elephant man.

"Better keep away from Mabel," replied the keeper. "She's got a bad tooth and is a little touchy."

They stepped into the long elephant room.

The air was close and heavy with the odor of animals. Dan's eyes became accustomed to the half light of the room and he gazed at more elephants than he had ever before seen at any one time.

"There must be fifty elephants in this barn," he exclaimed.

"There's not quite that many; only 43," replied the general manager.

"Do you take them all on the road?"

"Can't say yet. That will depend on just how many we need for the acts, but we probably will take the entire herd this year. A circus isn't a circus unless it has a lot of elephants and it will only require one more car in the train to take the complete herd. Last year we carried 36."

A small elephant decided to become friendly with Dan and he felt an exploring trunk nuzzling at his coat pockets.

"Sorry, young man," chuckled Dan, "but I haven't any peanuts today."

"Carrots make a bigger hit than peanuts," said Mr. Adams. "If you want to make friends with the herd, just bring out a couple of bushels of carrots."

Dan stepped closer to the small elephant and scratched its forehead. Suddenly he felt an elephant's trunk curl around his body. It tightened and his arms were held fast to his sides. He almost swallowed his Adam's apple as he was suddenly picked up and whirled through the air. Visions of being dashed to the hard floor of the barn flashed through his mind during his brief flight. Then he was lowered gently to the ground and his arms released.

Dan let out an involuntary squawk of relief and he heard the circus manager chuckling.

"That's just one of old Maude's jokes," explained Mr. Adams as Dan looked up at the largest elephant in the herd. "When any of the babies get too much attention Maude has a way of taking visitors for a ride."

"It certainly gives a fellow a scare," admitted Dan. "I saw myself being dashed to the ground and trampled underfoot."

"Old Maude could do that if mad enough, but we've never had an accident like that in the 17 years I've been running the Great United, and Maude has been leader of the herd all of those years."

"Has the herd always been this large?"

"I should say not. Old Maude was my first elephant in the days when I had a wagon show. If she ever gets too old for the road, I'll pension her and keep her at the farm. She's almost like a member of the family."

Dan noticed, as they left the elephant barn, that there was a large stove to warm the quarters if the temperature dropped too low.

In a second barn paralleling the first the cat animals were kept and they could be heard before seen.

"We've just got the big cats back from a tour on vaudeville," explained the manager as they went into the barn and Dan knew that he would soon be viewing at close range the animals Bob McMasters had worked on the stage of the Majestic the night before. This barn was better lighted than the elephant quarters, with rows of cages down each side. The cages were permanent, built into the wall of the structure, and much larger than the ones in which the animals were confined when out for the summer tour with the big show.

"There are more than forty lions and tigers in the menagerie and Captain McMasters, our chief trainer, plans to work most of them in his big act this summer.   I don't think McMasters is much older than you are, Dan."

"Not more than a year or two," agreed Dan. "We met last night in his dressing room at the Majestic."   He explained the circumstances of the meeting and how Fred's quick cry had saved the trainer from possible serious injury from the lion Jup.

"Well, that certainly is interesting," said Mr. Adams.   "If you join the show, you will see quite a lot of Bob and write a lot about him. His act is our big drawing card.   There's Jup over in cage No. 9 right now.   He doesn't look especially ferocious."

Dan observed Jup at closer range.   He was a tawny brute, a magnificent specimen of a lion, and he watched them through half closed eyes. When his curiosity had evidently been satisfied he rolled his head to the inner side of the cage and proceeded to go to sleep.

In another section of the barn was the special tank for the huge hippopotamus, Cleo, and in a third and smaller structure were the zebras and the giraffes, three of the latter gangly animals regarding them with distinct disfavor as they looked down on the visitors. "The trained ponies, the camels and the white cows from India are out on the farm," said Mr. Adams. "We can see them another time."

They left the barn and a short distance ahead Dan saw the private railroad siding which housed the train equipment of the Great United. Split into sections were the livestock, equipment and passenger cars and beyond them on another track was a miscellaneous collection of equipment.

"You've got a lot of railroad cars here at the farm," said Dan.

"There's enough to send out two forty car shows," replied Mr. Adams. "The first train is the Great United's equipment and that stuff on the other track represents cars I've picked up in various places in the last fifteen years. Most of them were in good shape and I got them for little or nothing. On two occasions smaller shows were stranded nearby and all I had to do was pay the freight bill to get them over here. I call that second track 'graveyard row' for there stand my own hopes of a second big circus."

"But if times improve you plan to put out

another show, I suppose, don't you?"

"I'm not counting on that too much. My only hope now is to get the Great United through the next season successfully. Either the Amalgamated or my own show will go under. We can't continue our present cut-throat competition and both survive."

In a low, rambling structure beside the rail-road spur Dan saw the wagons, drawn up in even rows. They were all clean but many in need of paint.

"The paint crew starts work next week," Mr. Adams explained. "From then on this is going to be a mighty busy place getting ready for the start of the season."

At the far end of the shed there was a collection of equipment under heavy canvas covers.

"The most beautiful parade wagons in the world are stored over there," said the circus manager. "We haven't carried them with the show in eight years but it wouldn't take more than a week to get them ready to parade again."

"That's one thing I miss about the modern circus," remarked the publisher of the Review. "I can remember when I was a youngster and

Barnum was touring the country with 'the greatest show on earth.' We lived 18 miles from the town where the circus was to appear and I was up at daylight worrying for fear we wouldn't get started early enough. The whole family went. It was the big event of the year. We had an early lunch in a grove just before we got to the city and arrived in time to see the parade. It was the thrill of my young life and I believe I actually enjoyed it more than the main show."

"I hated to see the parade go," admitted the circus manager, "but the cost of carrying the extra equipment on the train and then the fact that we had to make longer hops made it almost impossible for us to put on a parade and then get our equipment up in time for the afternoon show."

They walked slowly back toward the house and Mr. Adams led the way to his office on the first floor. The walls of the room were covered with circus lithographs.

"I've been working on the posters we'll use during the coming season," he explained, "which is another reason I need the help of a chief press agent at once."

"But I don't know anything about posters," protested Dan.

"As a newspaper man you should have a good idea of what appeals to the public," continued Mr. Adams. "If you decide to join us we would get to work at once on the posters, handbills, pictures and stories for the newspapers. You would find plenty to keep you busy until the show takes the road and after that I think I can assure you that you would have even more thrills and excitement than in your newspaper work."

"How about my assistants?" asked Dan.

"You will have a free hand in picking them," promised the circus manager.

"Would you have any objection to my taking some of them from the staff of the Review?" Dan asked the publisher.

"Well, I hadn't counted on that. How many would you want?"

"Probably two."

"I think that could be arranged."

Dan looked out the window at the circus farm. On every barn was the name, "Great United," and beyond them the railroad siding with the long string of cars waiting for spring and the start of the season.   The thrill of the circus was in his blood and when he turned back from the window he had made up his mind.

"I'm ready to start work now," he said.

Chapter V

THE NEW JOB

Following Dan's decision to join the staff of the Great United as chief press agent, there ensued a long conversation concerning the details of the work and the question of salary.

"What are we paying you on the Review as our star feature writer?" Mr. Benbow asked.

"I'm getting $50 a week."

"I'll add $10 a week to that," said the general manager. "Of course there is no cost for your board and room while you are out with the show since you will have a stateroom on the train and will eat your meals at the general dining tent."

"Now what about assistants? You said something a while ago about taking some of them from the staff of the Review," said the publisher.

"How many am I allowed?" Dan asked Mr. Adams.

"That depends somewhat on how much their

salary will be and how capable they are. Usually we have three men on advance press."

"If I can get the boys I have in mind I think two of them will be able to handle the job."

"Who are they?" asked Mr. Benbow.

"Fred Watkins, assistant sports editor, and Jack Mathews, who is on the night police run."

"Both good newspaper men," agreed the publisher. "As far as I am concerned they can join the circus and when they're through in the fall I'll see to it that there are places for them on the staff."

"I'll want you to join me here at once," said Mr. Adams. "There is a tremendous amount of detail to be taken care of before the show goes on the road. You'll have this small room to the right as your office. The one on the other side belongs to Guy Chappell, who serves as general booking agent and then as ringmaster when the season starts. He'll be back from the east soon with a lot of new acts lined up for the season."

Dan and the publisher of the Review returned to Ralston after it had been decided that Dan would finish his work on the paper that afternoon and report to the circus farm the next morning.

When they reached the editorial office, Dan went to his desk while Mr. Benbow stopped at the city editor's desk to inform Jackson that Dan was leaving the staff. Dan saw the city editor's face flush and he appeared to be protesting at the change. It was evident, however, that his objections were of little avail and after Mr. Benbow had gone into his private office the city editor stormed over to Dan's desk.

"What's this about you going with the circus?" he demanded.

"It's true enough," said Dan. "I'm to finish up work here this afternoon and report at the circus farm tomorrow."

"I call it a mighty dirty trick," said Jackson. "Here I get you trained into a real newspaper writer and then the boss comes along and steals you for his circus."

"Maybe he didn't tell you the whole story," said Dan. "What about Fred and Jack?"

"Well, what about them?"

Dan sighed, for he knew the city editor would hit the ceiling when he learned that the assistant sports editor and the night police reporter were to be given opportunities to join the press staff of the circus.

"I'm going to need two men on advance," explained Dan, "and Mr. Benbow said it would be all right for me to select a couple I knew from the Review's staff. I want Fred and Jack."

"Good heavens," exclaimed Jackson. "What am I running, a training school for circus press agents? Say, don't you want to take me along to water the elephants?"

"We won't all be leaving at one time," explained Dan. "It will be some weeks before I'll need Fred and Jack."

"What have they said about it?"

"Nothing yet. I haven't talked with them."

"Then I'm going to see them first. Maybe I can pound enough sense into their heads so they'll stick by the paper instead of gallivanting all around the country with a circus."

"You'll have to talk fast."

"So will you. Here comes Fred."

They called the assistant sports editor over to Dan's desk and Jackson managed to get in the first words.

"You're not thinking of leaving the Review, are you?" he asked.

Fred looked startled.

"What's the matter? Someone putting the blue slip in my pay envelope and letting me out into the cold, cruel world?"

"Not as far as I know," admitted the city editor. "By the way, you never did like circuses, did you?"

"Well, I can't say I have been particularly fond of them, but——"

Jackson turned triumphantly toward Dan.

"There," he said. "Now how much chance have you got to sign Fred on your advance staff?"

"Say, what's this all about?" demanded the perplexed Fred.

"Simply this," Dan explained. "I'm leaving the Review staff tonight to join the Great United in winter quarters as their general press agent. I'm going to need a couple of good assistants when the season starts and I want you and Jack to come along with me."

Fred's eyes lighted up with enthusiasm.

"You bet I'll go," he said enthusiastically.

"Now wait a minute," interjected Jackson. "I just asked you a minute ago whether you liked circuses and you gave me the idea that you didn't."

"I said I hadn't been particularly fond of them," Fred explained, "but you didn't give me a chance to finish. What I wanted to say was that after seeing Bob McMasters in his wild animal act and talking with him in his dressing room afterwards, I changed my mind about circuses."

"And to think that all of this sorrow comes from giving you a couple of passes to the Majestic," moaned the city editor. "Well, I've got one more hope. Maybe Jack will listen to a sane man."

"Jack's never had a sane moment in his life," chuckled Fred. "If he had he wouldn't be a night police reporter."

The city editor looked at them disgustedly and went back to his desk. For the next half hour he answered his telephones with a savage voice. Then he smiled. He couldn't blame the boys for jumping at the chance to join the circus and he could kick a year and it wouldn't do any good since the publisher now owned a substantial interest in the Great United.

Dan and Fred talked at length about the circus and Fred grew more enthusiastic as they talked.

"You say I'll probably be traveling ahead of the show?"

"We're only going to use two advance men this season," said Dan. "Jack will visit cities two weeks before the show arrives and you'll follow a week later. Then I'll come along with the show, plant the show day stories in the newspapers, entertain visiting reporters when they come down to the lot and see that the newspaper people have plenty of passes for after all they are a showman's best friends."

"It sounds great to me. The sooner spring and circus time arrive the happier I'll be."

Dan finished writing his story on the builder of the miniature locomotives and turned the copy in to Jackson.

"Dan," said the city editor, "I'm sorry to lose you but I know you will make a success of your new work. I expect this is the last story you'll write for the Review for a long time."

"Hardly. Remember that the Great United opens its season here and I'll be coming in every once in a while with a feature story."

"What if I refuse to run them?"

"No story, no passes."

"That's a real club. But don't worry, Dan,

I'll run all of the circus features you write for I know they'll be good.   And here's a tip to use in getting your publicity ready.   Don't make exaggerated statements in your stories.   The newspaper reading public of today is too intelligent to be taken in.   Write a good newspaper story and illustrate it with circus scenes. Animals will attract the youngsters and pretty aërialists will draw the older folks."

The city editor stood up and grasped Dan's hand firmly in his own.

"There'll be a job waiting for you as long as I'm city editor.   Good luck."

Dan returned to his desk, a queer mist in his eyes.   Jackson's words had brought home to him that he was definitely leaving the Review. He sat down at his desk and cleared out the few personal possessions it contained.   He wrapped them in a paper and walked slowly out of the editorial office.   As he went down the stairs the presses thundered into life with the final edition of the day and it was with a feeling of distinct sadness that Dan walked away from the home of the Review.

That night at dinner he broke the news to his father and mother.

"But, Dan," said his mother. "That means you'll be away from home all summer."

"I'm afraid it does, mother."

"Circus people are rough folks," she added. Dan's father spoke.

"Don't worry, mother. If Dan is with Hugh Adams' show you may be sure that his associates will be all right. Dan's old enough now to know how to pick his friends. I think it is a splendid recognition for your work. Go to it and make it a real success."

Later that evening Dan went down to the central police station where he found Jack Mathews dozing in a corner. Jack was willing to listen to almost any proposition that promised something out of the ordinary and it was easy for Dan to sell him on the idea of joining the Great United.

Jack was an ideal fellow for advance agent. He was large, with a great booming voice and a pleasant personality. When he got into a tight corner, he usually managed to talk his way out and Dan knew that circus men needed nimble wits.

"There'll be that little question of renumeration," Jack suggested.

"What are you getting now?"

"The munificient sum of $35 a week and they bury my talent in a dingy police station."

"Then I am safe in promising you $45 a week and expenses."

"When do we start?"

"That's a question I can't answer definitely. About the 25th of April."

On his way home that night Dan reviewed the sudden turn of events which in less than 24 hours had transformed him from a newspaper man into a publicity agent for the Great United. He had to pinch himself to realize that on the following morning he would take a suburban train for Coralville and his first day's work with the circus.

Chapter VI

THE SEASON STARTS

The following morning Dan journeyed to Coralville and was installed in the small office adjoining that of the general manager of the Great United. Mr. Adams spent most of the morning with Dan, explaining some of his early duties and at noon the new press agent was introduced to Mrs. Adams, a motherly woman who invited him to have dinner with them. Through the noon hour she recalled many interesting events which had happened in other years on tour for she usually accompanied her husband when the Great United was on the road.

In the afternoon Dan found several leisure hours and he visited the barns again where he met Bob McMasters.

"Hello, there," said the animal trainer. "I didn't expect to see you again this soon."

"Newspaper men have a habit of turning up unexpectedly," smiled Dan as they shook hands. "As a matter of fact, I've deserted the newspaper game and have joined the Great United."

"Fine. What are you to do?"

"The present label after my name is chief press agent but I'm still a little vague on my duties."

"You'll get onto the ropes soon enough. We need some more live wires like you on the show. I've got a hunch there is going to be plenty of trouble this season."

"What do you mean?"

"Didn't Mr. Adams tell you about the Amalgamated?"

"He said the two shows were rivals and that Barney Hutchinson was using every trick possible to damage the reputation of the Great United and put it out of business."

"Hutchinson is an all round rascal and we'll have to be on our toes every minute this season. The thing that worries me is the hunch I have that he's got some of his own agents still planted in our own show and some of them may be pretty high up in the organization. Last year he seemed to know all about our route even when it was kept as secret as possible and the

Amalgamated would pull in and play the same towns we did. Believe me that's expensive business for both shows."

"Do you suspect anyone in particular of giving away information to Hutchinson?" asked Dan.

"I'm not ready to say," Bob replied. "It would be too unjust to accuse a man on only a hunch."

They talked for a time, Bob explaining in detail the plans for his enlarged act during the coming season.

"I've got a black panther I'm trying to break into the routine," he said, "but he's a fierce brute and I'm having a hard time. After I get all of the lions and tigers posed, I want to turn this black brute loose in the arena and force him onto a pedestal to cap the climax."

"Won't that be too dangerous?"

"It may be but I'm going to give it a try. I hate to think I can't control the black brute."

"I'm going through the picture file from last year," said Dan, "and if I don't find the pictures of your act I need can you pose for some others?"

"Glad to. Publicity brings the crowds and

big crowds mean fat pay checks for yours truly."

Dan went down to the railroad yard and walked alongside the Great United's train. He came to the Pullman section with the string of bright red cars. At the far end was one marked office and he climbed up on the back platform and gazed through the full-length windows. This car was to be his home for the circus season. He rattled the door but found it locked. He would have to get the key and come down and investigate another day.

When he returned to the office, Mr. Adams handed him a telegram. Dan noticed it was from Chicago. It was addressed to the general manager and read:

"Home tomorrow morning. Greatest lineup of acts ever. Should mean wonderful season." It was signed by Guy Chappell, the booking agent and ringmaster.

"We'll actually get down to work tomorrow," said Mr. Adams. "Guy should have a lot of pictures and stories on the acts he has booked and you can get busy on your typewriter turning out copy."

Dan met the general agent the next morning at the office. He was a thin, wiry man, a bundle of nerves, but he was tremendously likeable and Dan felt that they would soon be good friends. With long, artistic fingers, the agent ran through the mass of material he had brought back, stopping now and then to select a photograph of some new act and exclaim on its merits.

"I've learned the feature of the Amalgamated's new bill," he said. "Picked up a straight tip in New York. Barney Hutchinson has booked a European daredevil for a cannon act and instead of being shot across the tent, this chap is going to be shot almost the length of the hippodrome track."

"Sounds like a sensational act," said Mr. Adams.

"Sure, but I've booked an Italian that has it backed off the map. Listen, to this. Our man, Bravo, ascends to the top of the tent. Then with his partner, a girl, clinging to his back, leaps into a short chute. At the end of the chute he soars into the air, a regular swan dive, headed for the ground. The only thing on which to land is a chute elevated about 10 feet above ground and set on an angle. He strikes the chute, slides down it, and comes to a stop. How's that for a thriller?"

"It can't be done," said the general manager decisively.

"It can be done for I saw it in New York. Believe me I couldn't get out a pen fast enough to sign Bravo to a contract. It costs shekels but it will be worth it. Here's a picture of Bravo and his partner."

Dan gazed at the pair who were to provide the aërial sensation of the show. Bravo was a swarthy little man with unusually large shoulders. His partner was a slender girl of not more than 20.

"Here's an actual photograph of the act snapped in New York," said Guy, producing a glossy print of Bravo, with the girl clutching his back, flying through space.

"It will be a tremendous sensation to close the show," said the general manager. "What else did you dig up in the east?"

"The finest tumbling act I've ever seen, a new troupe of Arabians, and when it comes to tumbling they're without peer. I actually got dizzy watching them in the gymnasium. Then I found a triple somersault artist nearly as good as Alfredo Codona and a high wire act that brought my heart into my mouth. There'll be more thrills under our big top this year than carried by any other circus in the country and I'm not barring the big one."

"Let's sit down and see just what we've got under contract," suggested Mr. Adams.

Dan retired to his own office with the portfolio of material Guy Chappell had brought. He ran through it, sorting out pictures and stories, and then set himself to the task of re-writing the stories.

Before the end of the week the general manager and the agent had pretty well decided on the routine of the new acts and how they would fit into the performance. Dan then selected pictures to be made into cuts, sent his stories out to a job printing office to have hundreds of copies printed and worked up press books for his advance agents, from which they would supply the newspapers with ample stories and pictures.

In the meantime the carpenters and painters were busy in the shop, hauling in wagons which needed repair and giving the entire train a fresh coat of paint. Throughout March there was an air of suppressed activity all over the farm.

Mac Herndon, the head elephant trainer, was exercising his bulls on every favorable day, putting them through all of their old tricks and developing a new routine for the coming season. Bob McMasters was working hard to get the black panther into the act, but he privately confessed to Dan that he would be in danger every time the panther sprang into the arena.

"You'd better give it up," Dan counselled his friend. "The act is enough of a sensation now that you're working 35 animals instead of 28."

"You're probably right," conceded Bob, "but it's more or less a point of pride right now and I can't bring myself around to quitting. That big black boy will probably claw me up before I'm finally convinced that he can't be used in the arena."

In the canvas shop, the tent maker and his assistants were busy getting the big top ready and waterproofing it. The stubby, powerful trucks which were used in pulling the huge canvas wagons were given thorough overhaulings and the electricians arrived to inspect the two huge light trucks and all of the intricate

electrical equipment which was a part of the
big show.

Spring was definitely at hand and the start
of the season only a few weeks away. Fred and
Jack were brought out to the farm and given
thorough instructions on their duties. The
chief contracting and routing agent, Mel Har-
der, was already busy picking out an early season route and the crews for the advance cars
were assembled. Jack was to travel with the
No. 1 car and Fred with the No. 2 outfit.

Circus posters appeared all over Ralston,
where the Great United opened, and every time
Dan went to the city he saw some of the pictures he had helped select plastered on the bill-
boards.

Guy Chappell had forsaken his duties as
booking agent and was devoting his full time
to the job of ringmaster, which on the Great
United consisted of a multitude of tasks for
on Guy's shoulders fell the responsibility for
a beautiful, smooth-running performance. He
worked out the pageant and set the time for
the various acts as the show progressed and it
was his whistle which ruled the hippodrome
after the opening fanfare of trumpets.

Only ten days remained before the show train rolled away from winter quarters. The Pullmans were opened and Dan started moving in his stateroom in the business car, which was most comfortably arranged. The main office was at the rear of the car and just behind it Dan had a small cubicle with a desk and type-writer where he could write feature stories for papers that could use them. Here he also kept a file of all publicity used about the circus. On the walls he posted the pictures of the featured performers.

Further back in the car were the staterooms, a double one for the general manager and his wife, one for the publisher of the Review when he cared to travel with the show and the re-maining two for Stanley Goodwin, the show treasurer and legal adjuster and Dan. The new press agent's stateroom was at the very head of the car. Into this he moved the cloth-ing he planned to take on the tour for the car was to be his home until the circus came back to Ralston in the late fall.

Performers started drifting out to the farm. Acrobats and tumblers, clowns and equestri-ennes, they came to renew old acquaintances and to make new ones. Despite the short haul from the suburb into the city, the train was to be used.

The canvas was given a final inspection and loaded into the huge wagons. The seat trucks were jerked away behind the chugging trucks and down to the train where horses, used on a special hitch, pulled the heavily laden vehicles up the incline and started them down the flat cars.

Dan, watching the proceedings, marveled at the ease with which the organization worked. Back on the practice lot Guy Chappell was putting the acts through their routine. The costumer was busy with final fittings of the garments to be worn in the opening pageant, "Song of the Nile," in which Cleopatra was featured.

Aërialists set their rigging and swung dizzily about. Tumblers whirled and spun and the clowns worked diligently on stunts that were to draw the smiles and chuckles from thousands of circus patrons.

Over in the animal barns Bob McMasters was putting the finishing touches on his act. The black panther had finally been worked into the routine and Bob felt safe in using him.

Old Maude, leader of the huge elephant herd, trumpeted proudly as her followers were put through their acts.

From morning until night the farm was alive with activity. On the day before they opened the season in Ralston, Guy Chappell ran the show through a complete performance, timing it with watch and directing it with his whistle. Dan, standing on the side, was thrilled at the manner in which the acts fitted together. They were troupers, every one, taking an almost consuming pride in their work, and the performance went off smoothly.

The loading of the train went on well after nightfall. Torches flared and smudgy oil pots threw faint flickers into the sky. Mr. Adams was everywhere, consulting the trainmaster, then talking with the ringmaster and the treasurer. Once he stopped for a few words with Dan.

"Great publicity work in the Ralston papers," he said. "We ought to have a record crowd tomorrow for an opener."

"I hope so for the show certainly deserves it.

"We're giving the people their money's

worth this season." Then the general manager was away to look after some other duty.

In mid-evening the publisher of the Review arrived to watch the final loading of the train. He was to travel with the show the first few days.

It was 11 o'clock before the last wagon was rolled onto the 38 car train and the torches were gathered up. The work horses trotted toward the horse cars and gradually silence descended on the long train. Lights in the Pullmans went out as performers retired. Finally there was only the gleams in the windows of the business car at the rear where a midnight conference was being held. The executives of the show were around the general manager's desk.

"We've got the highest class circus in the world," Dan heard Mr. Adams say as he slid into his chair outside the inner ring grouped close to the desk. "But in spite of the quality of our show, we're going to have another fight with the Amalgamated as you all know. I'm counting on every one of you to give me 100 per cent loyalty. With that I am sure the Great United will win. Without it, we might just as well stay in winter quarters. What do you say?"

Dan scanned the ring of faces. There was Guy Chappell, the ringmaster, Billy Duffy, the trainmaster, Stanley Goodwin, treasurer and legal adjuster, and Mr. Benbow. Beyond them stood Bob McMasters, Mac Herndon, the elephant trainer. They were not exactly executives, but they were a part of the show's official family and the general manager wanted them to know he was counting on their loyalty.

Dan's eyes paused as he came to Stanley Goodwin. The treasurer was thin of face and his small eyes were set far back in his head. There was something piggish about him that disturbed Dan.

The answer to the general manager's question was unanimous. He was informed in no uncertain terms that the show was with him in a fight to the end.

"That's all I wanted to know," he smiled. "Better get to bed, boys. It's going to be a busy season starting tomorrow."

Dan retired to his stateroom, leaving the general manager and the publisher conversing in the office. The press agent, tired from the long day, dropped into a heavy sleep. Sometime in the early hours of the morning an engine coupled onto the long train and pulled it around to the other side of the city. When daylight came Dan looked out on a new scene. The winter quarters were behind. The season was under way.

Chapter VII

BOB DISAPPEARS

Dan dressed rapidly and stepped out in the aisle. The car was apparently deserted and he hurried outside. The long, red train had been broken into four sections and the Pullmans were far down a long siding. Up ahead he could see the roustabouts unloading the equipment for the cook tent, the first wagons off the train.

Hostlers were busy leading the work stock out of the long cars, while the elephant men were guiding their lumbering charges down the inclined platforms. The usual crowd of small boys, with a goodly number of their elders, was perched along the railroad embankment watching the elephants.

Dan went up to the other sections where the unloading was now progressing swiftly. The lot was a mile from the siding and, as Mac Herndon put it, "just the right distance." They could keep the wagons rolling smoothly without having them pile up at the train as they did on short hauls, or have to wait for the trucks or teams on the longer pulls.

Dan had a number of duties to perform that morning and he hopped one of the canvas wagons as it rolled along behind a truck. The lot was a scene of amazing energy. The markers for the tents had been placed by the 24-hour man, who preceded the show by just that length of time to make sure that everything is in readiness for its arrival. Eight, twelve and even sixteen horse teams rolled the great wagons to their locations where the roustabouts were waiting to unload the equipment. The cook tent was up, trucks from town were delivering the necessary supplies and in less than an hour the flag fluttered over the dining tent, signifying that breakfast was ready.

The press agent went into the tent. Before him were long rows of tables and a strip of canvas divided it into two sections. The section to his right had table cloths on the tops while the tables to his left had paper coverings. A waiter approached.

"New to the show?" he asked.

"Yes," smiled Dan. "I'm the press agent."

"Then you'll sit at the executive's table," said the waiter, leading the way to the head table.

Breakfast was served at once but before Dan was through the tent was well filled. Practically everyone was strange until Bob McMasters, who as the star also rated a place at the head table, came in.

"Great day to open the season," he said. "When the weather is fine on the first day, I always figure we'll have a successful year."

"Here's hoping you're right."

An attractive girl entered and sat down on the other side of Bob. He greeted her cordially and turned to Dan.

"I want you to know Maja Manning, the best woman rider in the business," said Bob.

"You're the new press agent, aren't you?" asked the girl.

"Yes," replied Dan, who was struck by the girl's beauty and youth.

"I think you've been doing a splendid job. I've read every one of your stories in the local papers."

"Dan will do his best to get the crowds," said Bob, "but he told me the other day he thought the riding acts were going to be a little weak."

Dan flushed quickly.

"I said no such thing," he protested.

"I'm sure you didn't," replied Maja. "That's just Bob's idea of a joke."

"No harm done," grinned Bob. "We all concede you haven't got an equal as a rider."

Dan privately observed that it would be hard to find an equal for Maja's beauty. Her hair was soft and brown, her eyes the same rich color, and her cheeks a rich olive with just the slightest hint of color.

Breakfast over, Dan took a trolley into the city. He had feature stories for both the Review and the Times, describing the unloading of the train and the opening of the season. Also in his pocket was a large book of passes, which he disbursed liberally in the Review office. The Times also received a generous quota, for they had been helpful in running most of the stories he had sent in.

It was noon before Dan was back on the lot. The place had been transformed. The big top was up, the seats in place, the rigging up and ready for the afternoon show. In the

menagerie the elephants were being brought
into line and the camel herd was munching
contentedly on its hay.

Ranged along the other side were the cages
with Bob McMasters' lions and tigers. After
the show started, the runways would be opened
and the big brutes sent leaping into the steel
arena in the main ring.

The dining tent was crowded when Dan entered but there was a place for him at the head
table.

"Biggest down town seat sale we've ever had
on the opening day," Dan heard the treasurer
telling Mr. Adams. "We may have them on
the straw by the time the show starts."

"What does 'on the straw' mean?" Dan
asked Maja, who was at his left.

"That means a crowd so large it overflows
the seats and straw has to be placed along the
track."

Dan did a little simple arithmetic. The
usual capacity of the tent was 6,500 and if the
crowd was large enough to overflow onto the
track, it would mean around 7,000 for the afternoon performance.

Before he was through with his meal, the

band in the sideshow was blaring and the barkers were shouting the wonders of the curiosities on display inside. The midway was jammed with humanity and the ticket office in the white wagon was doing a rushing business. Already people were starting through the turnstiles into the menagerie and Dan took his place behind the ticket takers and near the pass gate. Beside him in a small leather bag he had reserved seat tickets sufficient to care for all of the press passes which had been issued. It was his duty to see that the newspapermen received good seats and to make them feel that they were honored guests of the circus.

Only a few of the newspaper crowd appeared for the afternoon performance. Most of them would come at night. Inside, the band started playing and Dan thrilled to the music. The crowd was streaming into the tent in seemingly endless numbers.

Bob, in his white duck uniform trimmed with gold braid, slipped up beside Dan.

"They're putting down straw already," he informed the press agent. "This is some crowd."

"Some circus," smiled Dan in reply.

As two o'clock neared, the crowd thinned
out and Dan folded up his bag and went back
to the padroom where the pageant was as-
sembling. The costumes were a blaze of color,
silks, satins and velvets of the best quality in
order to stand the hard use of a circus season.
Horses pranced and even the elephants seemed
anxious for the start of the performance. The
calliophone carried on while band members
scurried out of the tent and slipped into their
costume for the pageant. Guy Chappell's
whistle shrilled, the curtains parted, the band
blared, and the show was on.

Dan watched the procession of animals and
performers moving onto the track. He heard
someone call to him and turned to see Maja
wave as she went past astride King, the finest
high school horse the Great United carried. It
was Maja who later would ride King dancing
around the hippodrome backward, keeping
perfect time to the music and then send him
headlong over the high barriers. But King
seemed to enjoy it every bit as much as his
young rider.

Dan stepped inside and looked over the
crowd. Every seat was taken and several hun-

dred people were sitting on the straw which had been placed on the track. The general manager and the publisher of the Review were watching intently. The pageant over, the band returned to its platform and the show swung into its cadence, timed by the whistle of the ringmaster. How different the performance under the huge white top and the one Dan had witnessed the preceding day on the farm. There was a snap and grace now that had been lacking before.

The crowd hushed as the ringmaster announced Bob's act as "the greatest wild animal act carried by any circus in the world, Capt. Bob McMasters and his 35 man eating lions and tigers."

There was a tremendous wave of applause as Bob appeared. Then down the long runway came the first of the lions, charging into the ring. A dozen of them milled around as Bob let himself into the arena, his chair in one hand, whip in the other. Slowly but smoothly he worked. Dan watched Jup with anxious eyes for after the performance at the Majestic when the big brute had almost struck Bob, he would never trust him. One after another Bob worked the animals onto their proper perches. Finally 34 of them looked down at him. Then, at a quick signal, the large panther shot down the runway and into the cage.

Like a streak of night it flashed into the arena, its wicked paws lashing at Bob, who stood off the attack with his chair. Jup raised his head and emitted a roar that fairly shook the tent and the others joined in. The furor was terrific, but Bob worked calmly, reaching through the bars for another whip an attendant held ready. The panther, frightened by the crowd, was unruly and it took Bob five minutes to get it on its perch.

It was almost unbelievable that 35 of the huge jungle beasts were in the arena and Dan counted them. There was no mistake. The runway was opened and Bob sent them leaping toward it, while the applause of the audience echoed through the tent.

Dan found himself wet with perspiration and Bob stopped when he left the tent.

"You look like a ghost," he told the press agent. "What's the matter?"

"If I die of fright, my life will be on your head," Dan grinned weakly. "I almost had heart failure along toward the end when the panther got unruly."

"Don't worry about me," grinned Bob. "If the panther gets so I can't handle him I'll send him back to his cage."

The performance went on smoothly. Dan especially liked the aërial work of the Rancon troupe, with Paul Rancon doing a triple somersault that was almost too fast to see.

The high wire work of the Borellis was another thriller with a triple mount just under the top of the tent and without a net. Then came the smashing climax of the afternoon, the leap from chute to chute by Bravo with his partner, Mlle. Dubelle, clinging to his back.

Bravo, guarding his act, had refused to put it into the rehearsal the day before. He carried his own assistants to rig the chute and to help him prepare for the flying leap. The audience was silent, waiting for the climax. The band played softly with the undertone of the kettle drums.

Up under the top of the tent, Bravo prepared for the leap. Dan saw his partner, Mlle. Dubelle, a mere slip of a girl, grasp Bravo's special harness which protected the head and shoulders of the daredevil. The drums rolled steadily. All eyes were centered on the top of the tent.

Bravo poised for the leap into the first chute. Into the metal slide he plunged, the girl clinging to his back. There was a breathless pause. Out into space they shot, a human arrow, hurtling down at a dizzying speed. Bravo's arms were outstretched, his body rigid.

Dan closed his eyes. There was no net. It didn't seem possible that they could hit the chute below without being crushed by the impact. He heard the great sigh of relief that preceded the thunderous wave of applause. Bravo and Mlle. Dubelle were safe in the chute.

The band broke into a lively air. The first performance of the new season was over.

Outside candy butchers were busy hawking their wares. The band in the sideshow blared lustily but Dan returned to the train. He wanted to rest and relax for a few minutes. Before entering his own car he stopped in the pullman just ahead where Bob had a stateroom. The animal trainer was busy writing letters.

"See you at supper," he told Dan, and the press agent went on to his own quarters.

The next day would find them at Macon, an 85 mile jump, and the season would be well under way.   There was an afternoon paper at Macon and Dan sat down at his typewriter and pounded out a special story to offer to the editor.   By the time he had completed the feature, it was time to start back to the lot.

Entering the dining tent, he looked around for Bob.

"What's the matter?" asked Maja.

"I'm looking for Bob," explained Dan.   "He said he'd see me here at supper."

"He's probably fallen asleep in his room."

"Hardly.   I looked in when I left the train and he wasn't there."

"Then he'll be along shortly.   He probably stopped to have a look at his cats."

Dan sat down beside Maja and they talked of various things, of circus life and its glamour, comparing it with the nervous tension of a great afternoon newspaper.

"We're funny things—people," said Maja. "You see the bright side of circus life and it appeals to you while I'd give almost anything to be a newspaper reporter."

The crowd in the tent thinned out, but still

Bob failed to put in an appearance. Dan and Maja walked over to the menagerie and inquired about Bob.

"Haven't seen him since the afternoon show," said the head cat man. "He usually comes in before this."

"I'm beginning to worry about him," Dan confided to Maja. "This doesn't seem like Bob."

"You're sure he wasn't asleep in his stateroom?"

"Positive."

"Perhaps he's met some friends and is having dinner off the lot."

"But the cat keeper said Bob was usually here at this time."

"That's so," admitted Maja. "You don't think anything has happened to him, do you?"

Dan was silent for a moment, mulling over the warnings that had been sounded about the Amalgamated. Bob was the star of the Great United. If anything happened to him the Adams-Benbow show would be seriously crippled in drawing power. The thought that Bob might have been attacked or kidnapped on opening day hardly seemed credible but it pounded at Dan's mind with a growing sense of apprehension.

"You're thinking about the Amalgamated?" insisted Maja.

"Right. I'm wondering if they could have done anything to Bob."

"They're capable of doing anything to put the Great United out of business," said Maja, with just a hint of a sob in her voice.

"I'm going back to the train and make a thorough search," said Dan. "Then, if I can't find Bob, I'll report to Mr. Adams at once."

"Good luck," said Maja as Dan hurried away on his search.

Reaching the train, Dan climbed into the head pullman. With time for the opening of the evening performance nearing, the train was practically deserted. He went through car after car, questioning several porters who were still on the train. None of them recalled having seen Bob.

Dan reached the next to the last car in which Bob's stateroom was located. He went through this carefully, looking in the washrooms and all of the staterooms that were open. Where the doors were locked he pounded lustily.

The door of Bob's stateroom was open. On the small writing table in one corner was a neat pile of letters Bob had been working on in the afternoon. The interior of the room was in perfect order. There was no sign of a struggle or commotion of any kind.

Dan went into the business car where his own quarters were located. Lights in the office at the rear had been turned on and he found the general manager of the circus and the publisher of the Review in conference with Stanley Goodwin, show treasurer.

"Sorry to break in," said Dan, "but I've got to see Mr. Adams a minute."

"What is it, Dan?"

"Won't you come to my office?" urged the press agent.

The general manager nodded and excused himself from the others.

"What's on your mind?" he asked when they were in Dan's small office.

"I can't find Bob," explained the press agent quickly. "When I came back from the lot this afternoon he was in his stateroom writing letters and said he'd meet me at supper. He failed to show up and I went over to the menagerie but the head cat man said Bob hadn't been around there. Then I came back to the train. I've been through every car but there isn't a sign of him."

"He's probably had dinner off the lot," said the general manager. Then catching the worried look in Dan's eyes, he asked sharply. "Do you think something has happened to him?"

"It begins to look like something unusual has happened," said Dan. "There's always the Amalgamated and Barney Hutchinson to remember. Don't forget that Bob and his animal act are our star attractions."

"You mean——?"

"Exactly. I mean that if something happened to Bob now and we had to cancel his act it would cause a tremendous loss in popular appeal for the show."

"I should say it would. That would just about wreck us. Come on. We're going to the lot at once."

The manager explained the situation briefly to the publisher of the Review and the treasurer. Mr. Benbow was worried but Stanley Goodwin manifested little concern and more than ever Dan felt his dislike for the treasurer.

Mr. Benbow's car was parked nearby and they hastened to the lot, now ablaze with lights. The midway was jammed with people and a steady stream was pouring through the turnstiles into the main tent.

Dan hurried up to the pass gate. Some of his friends from the Review would be going through on passes and he might need their assistance. The first one he saw was Charlie McKnight, the day police reporter and one of the smartest newspapermen in the city.

"Charlie," called Dan, "I've got to see you a minute."

"Can't be bothered," grinned Charlie. "I've got a sack of peanuts to feed to the elephants."

"I'm not kidding," said Dan tensely. "Something's gone wrong on the lot. Our star, Bob McMasters, the wild animal trainer, has disappeared."

"He's what?" demanded the astonished police reporter.

"He's disappeared. As far as we know he simply vanished from his stateroom late this afternoon and hasn't been seen since."

"Then count me in on the hunt. Where do we start?"

"Word is being passed around the lot now to learn if anyone saw Bob leave the train. We'd better get over to the ticket wagon. The general manager will be there."

An excited group was back of the ticket wagon. Word of Bob's disappearance had spread like magic. Guy Chappell was audibly wondering what to do about the routine of the performance.

"You'll have to strike the steel arena now," said the general manager. "Explain that Bob is unable to appear tonight. If we locate him before the end of the show we'll put up the arena and put on the act."

The boss roustabout put in an appearance.

"What's the matter, John?" asked the general manager.

"One of my boys saw McMasters leave the train about five-thirty," replied the husky foreman. "I just thought you'd want to know."

"Which way did he go?" asked Dan.

"He started toward the lot. That was the last any of my men saw him."

Dan swung toward Charlie McKnight.

"At least we've got something to work on.

We'll go back along every step of the route
to the lot.   There's a half dozen hamburger
stands that have been put up for the day.   One
of them may be able to give us a clue."

Dan and Charlie hurried away, leaving behind them the lot blazing with light and filled
with the blare of the bands, and a worried
group of circus people.

Chapter VIII

THE RESCUE

Dan dropped the role of circus press agent. He was a newspaperman again and on the trail of a big story. At his side was the alert and tenacious Charlie McKnight, who had a reputation for knowing every street and corner in the big city.

After leaving the lot, they started questioning the proprietors of the lunch stands which had been erected for circus day.

"Looks like we're going to be out of luck," said Charlie after they had stopped at seven stands without securing any information.

"We'll keep at it until we get back to the train," Dan said.

The music of the bands had faded into the distance when they came to a brightly lighted stand on a corner less than three blocks from the train. The proprietor was a keen looking young fellow and he answered their questions readily enough.

"Five-thirty?" he said. "Sure, I was here at that time. It was kind of quiet and I wasn't doing much."

"Say," he went on. "There was a large sedan parked down the street a half block with three or four fellows in it. One of them came back here and bought some smokes."

"What did he look like?" asked Charlie McKnight.

"He was thin and dark. I especially remember his right hand was scarred as though it had been burned. I saw it when he handed me the money to pay for his smokes."

Charlie swung toward Dan.

"Know who that was?"

"No."

"Slim Crawford!"

Dan's face whitened as he heard the name. Slim Crawford was one of Ralston's toughest characters, a gangster who had been successful in eluding all of the police traps set for him.

"What else happened here about five-thirty?" Charlie asked the owner of the hamburger stand. "Did you see anyone from the show talking with the gang in the sedan?"

"I didn't pay much attention," confessed

the young man, "but I noticed one man who might have been from the circus. They stopped him and he finally got in their car and they drove away with him."

"That must have been Bob," said Dan. "What did he look like?"

"It was too far for me to get a good look at him. He wasn't as tall as you are but a good bit heavier."

"Did he seem to resist getting into the car?" asked the police reporter.

"Not that I noticed. Say, what's up?"

"I wish I knew," replied Charlie. "Thanks a lot for the information."

They walked across the street from the hamburger stand before giving vent to their own ideas and feelings.

"There's no question but what Bob was kidnaped," said Dan, "and I'm sure that the Amalgamated must have hired Slim Crawford and his gang to do the job."

"You're probably right," conceded Charlie. "Crawford would attempt almost anything if he was sure he would make money at it."

"Where are Crawford's usual hangouts?"

"I wish I knew."

"Then there isn't much chance that we'll be able to find Bob and get him back on the lot in time to do his act tonight," said Dan.

"Not unless a miracle takes place."

Returning to the lot, Dan informed the general manager what had taken place near the hamburger stand.

"It's a cinch that Bob was kidnaped by Crawford and his gang."

"Which means that money from the Amalgamated paid for the job," said Mr. Adams bitterly. "It looks like this is going to be a tough season."

The band swung into its overture and the opening pageant paraded onto the hippodrome track. Dan was thinking rapidly.

"How much time have we got to find Bob?" he asked.

"You mean in time for tonight's performance?"

Dan nodded.

"Get him here by 9:45 o'clock and we'll put on his act."

"Is there any chance that we can locate Bob by that time?" Dan fired the question at Charlie McKnight. The police reporter inclined his head doubtfully.

"There's not much chance but we can try."

Leaving the main tent, they made their way to a filling station where Charlie phoned the central police station and put in an alarm.

"We'll have every officer in the city on the lookout for that black sedan in 10 minutes," he said. "I'll get them to put the radio squad cars on the job, too."

Leaving the filling station, they took a taxi into town. A worried desk sergeant was waiting for them when they arrived at the police station.

"We've got a clue to your man," he said. "That car was wrecked on the road out to Urbandale. Doesn't seem to have been anyone hurt but the men who were in it have disappeared."

"That's a tough district. Anything can happen out there," said Charlie.

"A squad car is getting ready to go out," said the sergeant. "You fellows better go along."

Dan and Charlie climbed into the long, black touring car with two officers. They shot through the traffic and out onto the Urbandale road. Three miles from the heart of the city they came upon the wrecked car.

"We're not over half a mile from the lot," said Dan. "The accident must have occurred soon after they forced Bob into their machine."

They asked many questions from nearby shopkeepers, but most of them were foreigners and the information they gained was of little use. The better part of an hour had slipped away and Dan felt that the chances of finding Bob in time for the night performance were now exceedingly slender.

They scoured the neighborhood and Dan was about to give up the quest when something bright reflecting the rays of a streetlight caught his attention. He stopped and picked it up. It was a pearl handled knife with a silver plate inlaid on one side. There was something on the plate and Dan held it out in the light to read the engraving. The words he saw startled him.

"Bob McMasters," was the two words engraved on the knife. They were on the right trail. Bob had been in the car when it struck the light pole and he had evidently had an opportunity to drop his knife. Dan called to Charlie and the two officers.

"We're right at the head of alley 31," said

the oldest policeman. "This is the toughest district in the state and Slim Crawford's particular hangout when he's in trouble. It would take an army to find your animal trainer."

"I've got the army," said Dan. "You show me where Crawford has his hangout and I'll see that he is smoked out."

"It's the third building from the end on this side of the alley," pointed out the policeman.

"You fellows stay here and see that no one makes a break," said Dan. "I'll be back in a few minutes with plenty of help."

Jumping into the police car he sped to the circus lot. Bill Duffy, the giant trainmaster, was the first man he met and Dan quickly explained what was needed. Then he raced on to tell the general manager. Mr. Adams looked grave when Dan told him what he had in mind.

"Do you think you can get away with it?"

"The police will be in the background. They won't cause us any trouble unless there is a wholesale riot. They've never been able to get anything on Slim Crawford and if we can clean out his place they'll give us a silent vote of thanks."

"Go to it and I hope you can get Bob back

safe and sound in time for a performance tonight."

When Dan returned to the back lot a strange
sight met his eyes. Old Maude was in her
working harness and beside her were four other
of the biggest bulls in the herd. With them
were their keepers and in the background half
a hundred roustabouts, all armed with heavy
clubs, had rallied under the direction of Bill
Duffy.

The strange cavalcade moved silently off the
lot, Dan at the head with Bill Duffy and Mac
Herndon, the head elephant man, at his side.
The elephants padded behind them. They
chose side streets and reached alley 31 almost
without observation.

Charlie McKnight came out of the shadows.
"The gang's at Crawford's place," he said.
"I got close enough to hear them talking. There
isn't any question but what they've got your
animal trainer."

Dan had worked out his plan of attack. Old
Maude and Bimbo were assigned to the front
of the building while the other three bulls
were stationed at the rear. When Mac Herndon blew his whistle they were to rush against

the lower section of the building, in which the gang leader maintained a fake pawn shop.

The whistle shrilled and a face appeared at the second floor window. Dan saw the man look down in astonishment and he heard a startled cry of alarm as old Maude put her sturdy shoulder against the front of the building and walked into the pawn shop. Bimbo was close behind her. From the rear of the building came the crashing of timbers as the three big bulls back there joyfully entered the destructive game. Mac Herndon stopped the attack and Dan cupped his hands and called to the men upstairs.

A man looked down at them and Charlie nudged Dan.

"That's Crawford himself," he whispered.

"What's going on down there?" demanded the gang leader.

"This is just a sample of what will happen if you don't turn Bob McMasters loose," replied Dan.

"I don't know what you're talking about," said the leader of the gang.

"Oh, yes you do," insisted Dan. "A few hours ago you kidnaped the animal trainer of the Great United. We're here to get him and we'll tear your place down if you don't turn him over in a hurry."

"You fellows are crazy. We'll have the cops on you in five minutes."

"The police think this is a fine picnic," replied Dan. "Either you bring Bob McMasters down in two minutes or we'll turn the elephants loose again and send a couple of tigers up the stairway for good measure."

"You wouldn't dare," cried the gangster and Dan could see his courage fading rapidly.

"Mac," he shouted to the elephant keeper. "Turn old Maude and Bimbo loose again. They ought to be able to shake those rats out of their perch in a few minutes."

Maude and Bimbo went to the task with a vengeance. Show cases inside the pawn shop were smashed, the stairs went crashing down, and the whole building shook.

Crawford reappeared at the window.

"We're coming down," he shouted. "Stop those elephants."

Herndon ordered Maude and Bimbo to cease their fun and the gangsters appeared at the head of the splintered stairway. Crawford was in the lead and behind him stood Bob.

Old Maude, feeling cheated at being unable to complete the destruction of the shop, reached up and jerked the gang leader off the stairs. He landed heavily on the floor and the herd leader curled her trunk around him, held him in a tight embrace, and swung him aloft.

"Stop it, Maude, stop it!" cried Herndon.

The elephant obeyed, lowering the white-faced gangster to the floor. Then she reached up and brought Bob down, carrying him gently and surely.

"Are you hurt?" Dan demanded.

"Not a bit," replied Bob. "They treated me well enough. Say, how far is it to the lot?"

"Less than half a mile. If you hurry you can get there in time to put your act in. It's 9:30 now and Mr. Adams said he'd put on the act if you got back by 9:45."

"I'm on my way," said Bob, departing on a run.

At a signal from Dan, Bill Duffy gathered up his roustabouts and started them back to the lot while old Maude picked the other gangsters off their isolated perch and lowered them to the floor.

"You're going back to the lot with us," he told Slim Crawford.

"I'm not going any place," said the gang leader, his courage returning.

Old Maude took a hand in the proceedings and almost before Crawford had the words out of his mouth he was in the tight embrace of her trunk. She swung him upward and then trotted down the alley following Mac Herndon.

"We'll take care of Crawford," Dan told the policemen who had remained in the background. "You can do what you want to with these fellows."

Despite the terrified protests of the gangster, old Maude carried him every step of the way back to the lot where he was finally deposited on the back lot. The general manager and the publisher of the Review were waiting for them.

"Take her away, take her away," moaned Crawford, pointing to old Maude, who was watching his every move through her tiny eyes. "She'll kill me."

"It might save the state a lot of trouble if she did," said Mr. Adams. "How much did the Amalgamated pay you for kidnaping our animal trainer?"

"I never heard of the Amalgamated," replied Crawford and there was a ring of truth in his words. "If you'll let me get out of this place alive I'll tell the whole story."

"Go ahead," said the publisher of the Review.

"I got $2,500 for the job," explained the gangster. "We were to get McMasters out of the way and then get an extra $500 for every week we held him captive."

"Who paid you the $2,500?" demanded the general manager.

"He said his name was Everett. I don't know where he was from or what his idea was. He offered me plenty of cash to do the job and I did it."

"Can you describe Everett?"

"There wasn't anything unusual about him. He was kind of thin-faced with small eyes and he's getting a little gray above his ears. He paid in cash."

Mr. Adams and Mr. Benbow drew aside and conferred for a few minutes. From the heavy applause coming from the main tent Dan knew that Bob was putting on his thrilling act.

"We've made up our minds about your case," the general manager told the gangster. "In the morning Mr. Benbow will report this incident to the district attorney and you may be sure that an indictment will follow. It will not, however, be served as long as you do not molest this show further. If we have any more trouble with you the indictment will be served and I can promise you that all your political pull will not save you from severe prosecution."

"You don't need to worry about me bothering this show anymore," said Crawford. "I've learned a lesson tonight."

The gangster faded into the night and Dan turned to Charlie McKnight.

"Sorry you missed the show, Charlie."

"I'm not. I was in on a private performance that beat anything in the big tent. When I write the story of how old Maude and Bimbo walked into Crawford's place and wrecked it he will be laughed out of town. What a story."

"Better come in and see the finish of the show. It will stand your hair on end."

The main tent was jammed to capacity and Bob was finishing his act when they entered. The black panther sprang to its place in the pyramid and the audience thundered its approval.

The cadence of the drum quickened and the lights went low as Bravo and his partner ascended the rigging in the center ring and prepared for the dive for life. Spotlights played on them and the crowd held its breath. Dan felt Charlie gripping his arm.

Bravo plunged downward, the beautiful Mlle. Dubelle clinging to his back. Out of the first chute they rocketed and into the air. Then into the second chute and safety.

The band blared, the lights came on, and the show was over.

Chapter IX

THREATS

The long red train of the Great United was creeping out of the Ralston yards that night when a grim-faced group gathered in the private office of the general manager.

Bob was there. So was Stanley Goodwin, show treasurer, and Mr. Benbow. Mr. Adams and Dan were the others.

"Let's hear the report for the day's business," said the general manager.

Goodwin consulted his balance sheet and announced that 13,321 people had seen the show during the afternoon and evening.

"That's a record for opening day," nodded the general manager. "Go on."

Expense items were quoted by the treasurer and when he had concluded and struck his balance it showed that the Great United had opened the season with a splendid profit.

"That's a wonderful report," said Mr. Benbow. "If we only keep near those figures."

"We'll make a good showing if we can keep the kidnapers and other thugs that Barney Hutchinson will hire off our lot," said the general manager. Turning to Bob, he fired a series of questions in rapid order.

"Did Crawford and his gang make any mention of the Amalgamated? Do you know who offered Crawford the money? What were they going to do with you?"

To the first two Bob answered in the negative but the third question brought some information.

"I heard them say they would take me out to a cottage on Crystal lake," explained the animal trainer.

The general manager was silent for a time. When he spoke it was with great deliberation.

"Hutchinson has showed his hand on our opening day and it will be a bitter feud this year; far worse than what we went through last season if what has taken place today is an indication. I'll send out word tomorrow to everyone on the payroll that we expect them to stand by the show. Bill Duffy and Mac Herndon can be counted on to keep their eyes open and they may be able to learn if anyone on the lot is trying to turn us into Hutchinson's hands. In the meantime, everyone keep on his toes."

They started to leave the office when the general manager called to Bob.

"I don't want you alone at any time," he said. "Your act is our main feature and I have not the slightest doubt but what the Amalgamated may try again to have you kidnaped."

"I'm going to carry a gun with me from now on and it won't be loaded with blanks," promised Bob.

"That's a wise precaution but I'm not going to leave you unguarded. Dan has a spare berth in his stateroom. I wish you would bring your things back in this car and double up with him."

"I'll be glad to," promised Bob. "After tonight's experience I agree that almost anything is likely to happen this season."

Dan and Bob left the private office together and made their way to the head end of the car. The train was well under way and the trucks clacked rhythmically as the long special rumbled through the night.

"I'll go up and get some things for tonight,"

said Bob, "and then finish moving in with you in the morning."

The animal trainer entered Dan's stateroom a few minutes later with his pajamas and toilet kit.

"I'm not in favor of kidnapings as a daily occurrence," he grinned, "but when they get me a roommate like you I don't object."

"That goes for me, too," smiled Dan. "I'm still mighty green about the show and I'll rely on you to help me a lot."

They prepared for bed and Bob rolled into the top berth, insisting that the air up there was better.

"I've trouped long enough to know the best berth," he chuckled.

Despite their fatigue, they talked at great length of the exciting events of the night.

"What happened when they kidnaped you?" Dan wanted to know.

"I fell into their trap almost too easily. I had left the train and was on my way to the lot. One of the gang was at the wheel of the car and the others were standing on the curb. One of them was trying to light a cigarette and couldn't seem to find a match. It was Crawford. He turned toward me as I came along and asked for one. That gave him a chance to come up close. When I replied that I didn't smoke and consequently didn't have matches with me, he told me to get into the car, that they would give me a lift to the lot. When I refused and told them I preferred to walk for the exercise, Crawford stuck a gun against my side. After that I didn't argue for I could see that the others had their hands on guns in their pockets."

"What about the wrecked car?"

"They drove around for a while and then started for Crystal Lake. A truck coming out of a side-street caused the accident. Our driver missed the truck but went into the curb and wrecked the car. Fortunately for Crawford it was near his hangout and they took me over there. By that time they were a little careless and I managed to drop my knife. After that there wasn't anything exciting until old Maude and Bimbo started walking through the front of the building."

"Dropping your knife was what gave us the clue to your whereabouts," explained Dan. "The policemen told us about Crawford's hangout and I hurried back to the lot and got a gang together."

"It looked like a young army. Those gangsters are nervy when they have everything their own way but old Maude and the rest of the elephants were too much for them. Crawford's mouth dropped open and he turned white when he felt the building start to shake and heard those big brutes tramping around down below."

"It's too bad that you couldn't learn who paid Crawford the money for your abduction."

"I'm convinced that it was someone connected with our own show. How would they know that it is my custom to walk back to the lot for exercise just before the evening meal?"

"That's true," conceded Dan, "but I'd hate to think of anyone in our own organization stooping that low."

"Well, you can bet your hat that there are some on the payroll who will do just such a thing."

"You want to take Mr. Adams' advice and see that someone is with you all of the time," said Dan. "If they kidnap you again they may have better success. That would not only stop our big act but ruin the morale of the whole circus."

The special clattered over a cross-over at a junction and Dan and Bob finally dropped asleep.

When morning came they were in the yards at Macon for the second stand of the season. They made their toilets and dressed leisurely. There was still ample time to reach the dining tent before breakfast was over.

"I forgot a tie I want to wear today," said Bob. "I'll run up to the car ahead and get it."

When Bob returned several minutes later Dan could see that something had upset him greatly. Bob handed the press agent a half sheet of plain white paper. There were several sentences in heavy black ink scrawled across the surface. Dan read it quickly.

"McMasters. We didn't get you tonight but we won't miss the next time. Keep that guy Tierney out of the way or he'll get hurt. You'd better get off this show and stay off if you know what's good for you."

Chapter X

THE MAN IN THE AISLE

Dan read the threatening note twice before he looked at Bob. There was an amused, quizzical look in the eyes of the animal trainer.

"I found that in my old room," he explained. "I wonder if anyone thinks they can frighten me by a childish note like that?"

"Perhaps it isn't as childish as it sounds," said Dan. "I'm beginning to believe that the Amalgamated is more dangerous than we have given them credit for being."

"Oh, it's a tough outfit all right, but we'll beat them in the end," said Bob confidently.

"Did you lock your room last night?"

"Why sure." Bob stopped suddenly. "And say, it was locked this morning."

"Then that means that someone on the train has a key to your stateroom and used it during the night. It's a good thing you came down and slept in my room or you might be among the missing this morning."

"What shall we do about the note?"

"Better give it to Mr. Adams. Then we'll stick together and I have a hunch we'll be able to take care of any trouble coming our way."

"I'm going back to my room to get a gun. Come along and we'll go down to the lot and see Mr. Adams."

Bob stopped at his stateroom where he delved into a battered traveling bag. Dan glimpsed several revolvers inside.

"Carrying an arsenal?" he asked.

"Most of these are guns I use in the act for firing blanks," explained Bob. "But this automatic I carry in my holster is capable of doing a lot of damage."

"Better look at your clips."

Bob broke the gun open. A low whistle escaped his lips.

"This is a fine mess," he exclaimed as Dan leaned over his shoulder. "Someone filled this gun with blanks for I always carried it loaded. It's the gun I have in my holster. I've never had to use it yet in the arena but there might be a first time. If I hadn't discovered the blanks just now I might have found myself in a tight place some afternoon."

"Whoever came in here last night and left the note must have tampered with your gun," said Dan. "Lay it down carefully. I've got a hunch that is worth following through."

Bob laid the gun down and Dan pulled a clean handkerchief from his pocket. He picked up the automatic and wrapped it in the piece of linen.

"What's the idea?" asked Bob.

"I'm going up town within an hour to call at the newspaper office and I'll just drop around to the police station. Macon is large enough to have a fingerprint expert on the staff. We'll see if we can get any prints besides your own from the gun. If we can they may come in handy one of these days."

Dan stowed the gun away in the pocket of his coat and they left the train. Far up ahead the unloading operations were well under way. The lot at Macon was less than half a mile from the tracks and they anjoyed the morning walk through the brisk air. The proverbial crowd of small boys was on hand when they reached the lot and a number of them had found employment carrying stakes and helping unroll and lace the canvas for the big top. The breakfast flag was flying over the dining tent and they found the general manager at the executive's table. They sat down opposite and took turns at relating the events of the morning, starting with the discovery of the note and concluding with the plan of having the gun finger-printed.

"How many know of your finger-print plan?" asked Mr. Adams.

"Only Bob and myself," said Dan.

"See that no one else learns about it. If you get any results it may be a most important key to the secret of who is directing the attack against the Great United for I am now thoroughly convinced that someone on our own train is close to Barney Hutchinson and working hand in hand with him to bring about the collapse of our show. I'm relying on you two to keep your wits about you and you may see something that is not intended for your eyes."

After breakfast Bob went over to the menagerie to see that his big cats were all right and then joined Dan for the walk uptown.

By the time they reached the railroad tracks the train was practically unloaded and a puffing switch engine was shunting the long string of red flat cars off the main line and onto a siding.   On every hand were posters and hand-bills proclaiming the greatness of the circus and the splendor and daring of the attractions.

The Macon Telegraph was a large and pros-perous afternoon daily and Dan found the city editor an alert, aggressive newspaperman. When he explained that he had left the staff of the Ralston Review only a short time before, Dan was welcomed with open arms.

"What's the story that came in on the AP this morning about an attempt to kidnap your star animal trainer?" asked the city editor.

"The kidnaping report was true enough," smiled Dan.   "Perhaps you would like to meet Bob McMasters, who was the victim of the attempt."

The city editor called a feature writer and for half an hour they plied Bob and Dan with questions.

"This is the best circus story we've ever had," enthused the city editor.   "Now if you've got a picture of McMasters we'll use it on the front page."

Dan opened his portfolio of publicity material and produced a picture of Bob posed with Jup.

"Incidentally," explained Dan, "the lion there tried to kill Bob several months ago when he was playing on a vaudeville circuit."

"I thought newspaper work was the most exciting thing in the world," grinned the city editor of the Telegraph, "but after what's happened on your circus the last 24 hours I've changed my mind."

"I'm going around to the police station," said Dan, "and I'd like to have you give me a note to the head of the detective bureau."

"What's up now?" the city editor wanted to know.

"Sorry I can't tell you," smiled Dan. "It's probably a wild goose chase but it is something I'm taking a long chance on."

The city editor scrawled the desired note and Dan and Bob left the office, directing their steps down the street to the police station, a scant two blocks away.

"From the standpoint of publicity," said Dan, "I wouldn't mind seeing you kidnaped about once a week."

"If it was a nice, pleasant kidnaping I

wouldn't object," grinned Bob, "but some of them might get a little rough."

The note from the city editor of the Telegraph gave Dan an open door to the office of the detective chief, a bulky Irishman named Wilkinson.

The press agent explained what had happened aboard the train and produced the gun, still carefully wrapped in the handkerchief.

"Sure, we'll be glad to see what we can find," said the detective chief. He summoned his fingerprint expert, who deftly took impressions of Bob's hands.

"It will be afternoon before the prints are developed," said the chief, "but if you'll come around after your afternoon show we may have something for you."

"Planning on seeing the performance?" asked Dan.

"I hadn't figured on it."

Dan pulled out his personal pass book.

"How many in your family, chief?"

"Well, there's the missus and three youngsters."

Dan tore out five passes.

"We've got the highest class circus in the

world," he said. "These passes are for the center section, the best seats in the tent."

The detective chief beamed his appreciation.

"Thanks a lot, boys. I'll certainly be there."

It was nearly noon when they returned to the lot, which had been transformed into a magic city during their absence. The big top was up and the gangs were placing the last of the seats. The rigging was in place and the animal cages had been rolled into the menagerie. The work horses had been fed and their harness loosened. Roustabouts were lounging in the shade. They had made an excellent run from Ralston to Macon and, with an early unloading, the work on the lot was completed well in advance of the usual time.

Dan sat beside Maja Manning at lunch that noon.

"I heard all about your rescue of Bob last night," she said, "but you disappeared this morning and this is the first time I've had to tell you what a splendid thing you did."

"Finding Bob meant just as much to me as the rest of you," replied Dan. "He's going to bunk with me from now on."

"That will be much safer. The lot has been

buzzing all morning with excitement over the events of last night."

The noon meal finished, Dan took his place at the entrance to the big top. For the better part of an hour he was busy honoring the passes which were presented and in return handing out reserved seats. The detective chief and his family arrived just before the start of the afternoon performance.

"Our fingerprint man got some fine pictures of the prints on the gun," he told Dan. "The proofs will be dry by the time the show is over. I'll take you up town with me."

The crowd that afternoon at Macon was not as large as the opening day throng at Ralston had been, but there were better than 5,000 people in the tent and General Manager Adams smiled as he checked over the receipts with the treasurer.

"We're getting away to a fine start," said Goodwin as he finished checking the money.

"I wonder how the Amalgamated is getting on?" the general manager asked the question half to himself.

"You ought to have someone on their show to keep you informed," urged the treasurer.

"I don't play the game that way."

Bob's act with the big cats and Bravo's thrilling leap brought ovations from the crowd.

When the show was over Dan waited at the pass gate for the detective chief.

"My home's only a short distance from the lot," he explained. "The folks will walk over."

"Great show you've got," commented the chief as they drove uptown. "It's no wonder your management worries about that trainer. The leap for life is good but for honest thrills I'll take that lion and tiger cat. Say, I wouldn't get in that steel arena if you gave me half of the city."

"It takes real nerve," agreed Dan.

When they arrived at the police station they found the prints taken from the automatic already on the chief's desk. The detective scanned the photographs. He handed one set to Dan.

"This set corresponds with the prints we took this morning from McMasters' hands," he explained. "The second set belongs to someone else. They're good and clear. Find that hand that made these prints and you'll know who tampered with the gun."

"We'd have to go through the entire show," said Dan, "and at present we haven't a shred of evidence against anyone on the train."

"Keep your eyes open. He'll slip one of these days and this set of fingerprints may prove invaluable when it comes to pinning the evidence on the right man."

Dan thanked the chief for his assistance, tucked the photographs under his arm, the gun in his pocket and went out to buy a copy of the Macon Telegraph. The picture of Bob and the story of the thrilling adventure of the night before was spread all over the front page. Dan chuckled as he read it. They should have a fine crowd for the night show.

Before returning to the train, he stopped at a book store, purchased a sturdy manilla folder, and a seal and stick of sealing wax. When he reached his own stateroom he found it un-occupied. He closed the door, bolted it on the inside, and sat down to work.

Placing the photographs of the fingerprints inside the folder, he carefully sealed the heavy manilla envelope. When he had completed his task he felt sure that it was practically im-possible for anyone to open the folder, extract the contents, and reseal the package without leaving tell-tale signs.

Dan turned toward the door to unlock it when a slight noise in the aisle caught his attention. He listened intently. There was the sound of cautious footsteps.

The press agent unbolted the door, flung it open and stepped into the aisle. There was no one in sight. He hastened into the vestibule and looked into the car ahead. Apparently there was no one there and he looked along both sides of the train.

Distinctly puzzled, Dan went back into the business car. Someone was shuffling through papers in one of the offices toward the rear and the press agent hurried down the car. He found Stanley Goodwin in his office. The treasurer looked up. He appeared surprised.

"Hello, Tierney. What's on your mind?"

"Did someone just come through and go out the back end of the car?"

"I didn't hear anyone. My back has been to the door but they would have had to move mighty quietly to get past."

"I had been working in my room," said Dan,

"and thought I heard someone just outside my door."

"Did you try the front end?"

"I looked there first but there was no trace of anyone."

"That deal last night was mighty queer," said the treasurer, leaning back in his chair, his eyes appraising Dan coolly. "You didn't stage it just for a publicity stunt, did you?"

Dan's cheeks flamed.

"I don't need to do anything like that to put the show across as far as the newspapers are concerned."

"Then you believe the story Slim Crawford told about being paid to abduct McMasters and hold him prisoner."

"I see no reason to doubt it."

"I wouldn't believe anything a fellow like Crawford said."

"He was pretty badly scared last night."

"I don't care whether he was scared or not. I wouldn't believe him."

"I can see you're determined not to. I don't suppose you believe Hutchinson and the Amalgamated have men planted in our outfit just to cause us trouble and attempt to force us in off the road."

"There's been lots of talk about that. I'd like to see a proof."

"We've only been out on the road a little more than 36 hours. It would take fast work to show you any definite proof in that length of time."

"I'm just as anxious to catch the trouble makers, if there are any, as you," said the treasurer. "Anything suspicious that comes up, let me know."

Dan nodded and returned to his own state-room. The folder which contained the finger-print photographs was intact and he sat down on his berth to think over the events of the last 24 hours.

First there had been the abduction of Bob, then the tampering with his automatic and finally the cautious steps outside Dan's door. The press agent went into the aisle and looked at the carpeted floor in front of his door.

The car had been cleaned after their arrival in the morning but an afternoon breeze had sent clouds of dust scurrying through the rail-road yards. There was a mantle of dust over

everything again.   Bending down, Dan scru-
tinized the carpet.   He couldn't be sure but he
thought he saw imprints which might have
been made by the knees of someone kneeling
at his door.

To make sure, Dan pulled the door shut.
He had bolted the door on the inside while
working with the seals on the folders.   There
had been no key in the lock.

From his position in the aisle he could peer
through the keyhole and into his own room.
To be sure the range of vision was limited but
it was sufficient to confirm his suspicions that
someone had been kneeling before his door.
Anyone in that position could have observed
him placing the photographs in the folder and
sealing them.

The realization that he had been observed
startled Dan.   Evidently the agents of the
Amalgamated had marked him as one worth
watching and the secret of the fingerprints was
no longer a secret.

There was a good half hour before supper
was served on the lot and Dan decided on a
hurried trip uptown.   Slipping the sealed
folder under his coat, he stepped off the head

end of the car and hurried toward the passenger depot. There he hailed a cab and sped uptown. Journeying to the bookstore he had patronized before he purchased a folder identical with the first and several sheets of stiff cardboard which he had cut to fit the manilla envelope.

Dan returned to within a block of the train in the cab. Walking the rest of the way, he was fortunate enough to find that Bob was still on the lot. This time he closed the door of his room, shot the bolt and stuffed the keyhole full of paper.

Working swiftly, Dan placed seals on the second envelope until it looked exactly like the first. When he had completed that task, he pulled the paper out of the keyhole, unlocked the door and carried the first envelope down to his office where he secreted it in a bottom drawer of his desk under a pile of newspaper mats.

Dan returned to his own stateroom, picked up the fake envelope, and started for the lot. The dining tent was well filled. The general manager was seated at the head of the executives table and Dan stopped beside him.

"I've got a folder I'd like to have you keep in the safe for me," he said.

"Certainly Dan," smiled Mr. Adams.

Dan was not displeased to note that many in the tent noticed him handing the folder to the general manager.

Chapter . XI

ON THE REAR PLATFORM

Dan was in the office in the business car that night after the show was over and he saw the general manager twirl the dials on the safe, open the door, and place the heavily sealed folder in an inner compartment.

"This must be pretty valuable," smiled Mr. Adams, "from all of the seals you've put on the outside."

"It may prove unusually valuable," said Dan.

Leaving the office, he went to his stateroom where Bob was undressing.

"Where were you hiding out this afternoon?" asked the animal trainer. "I looked all over the lot for you."

"I went uptown with the detective chief. By the way, here's your automatic."

Bob took the gun and slipped it under his pillow. A switch engine nosed against the string of pullmans and shoved them forward to couple on to the rear of the main train. They clacked slowly over the switch points and finally came to a stop near the passenger depot. Dan looked out. The usual throng was lined along the tracks watching the loading of the long train.

"I'm not sleepy," said Dan. "I'm going out and watch the crowd and the loading."

"Go ahead. I had a real tussle getting all of the cats on their perches tonight. I'm going to hit the hay right now."

Bob rolled into bed and Dan left the car. The night air had grown chill and he pulled his coat closer. Up ahead acetyline torches furnished the light for the loading.

The trucks chugged up the slope from the lot, pulling behind them the heavy wagons loaded with the canvas of the big top and the seats. The instant the truck cut loose, an eight horse team was hooked on to jockey the wagon into position before the runways. Then up the steel chutes the heavy vehicle rolled and onto the flat car to be trundled along to its proper place on the train. Under the watchful eye of Bill Duffy, the trainmaster, the task went on smoothly and rapidly. The arrival of a midnight mail train caused a temporary halt but by one o'clock the last wagon was in place. Men hurried along the side of the train picking up the torches and putting them aboard. The hulking freight engine that was to pull them to the next stop 105 miles away coupled onto the front end. The air was tested, lanterns waved along the train, and with a series of jerks the Great United's train got in motion.

Bill Duffy hurried up.

"Get on the back end with me," he said.

The pullmans slid by and as the business car came along Dan swung up on the rear platform. Bill followed, his lantern swinging a highball to the engineer far ahead. Answering blasts from the whistle indicated that the signal had been seen and the speed of the long train increased.

"Air's getting cold," said Bill. "I'm going up ahead. See you in the morning."

"Good night, Bill."

The door closed and the press agent was alone on the platform, watching the lights of Macon fade into a dull aura of light on the horizon. Finally they vanished and the train rushed through the night, the trucks playing their steady symphony over the steel.

The noise of the train drowned out any other sound but some premonition of danger crept into Dan's mind. He turned quickly toward the door. A shadowy figure loomed beside him. Something struck Dan a glancing blow on the chin. He slipped and fell to the floor.

Half dazed by the blow and the shock of his fall, he tried to rally his senses. His unknown foe was leaning toward him, his figure silhouetted against the sky. Dan saw an arm raised to deliver another blow. Mustering his strength he rolled aside just in time. Reaching upward he clutched desperately at the coat of his assailant.

Dan struggled to his feet but before he could straighten up a sharp kick in the stomach almost put him out of the fight. He cried out in agony at the pain but he managed to swing his right fist in a wild blow that caught his foe unaware.

Dan's mighty clout sent the other reeling against the railing on the far side of the platform and gave the press agent a chance to regain his wind and strength. The respite was only momentary. The unknown was at him like a tiger, fists flailing and feet flying.

A hard blow to the chin staggered Dan and he dropped his guard. Blows rained on his face. The other man was shorter but there was a viciousness about his attack that astonished Dan. He felt sure that in the end he would win the fight but it was going to be a battle.

Dan settled down to a methodical fight. While fists were hammering his cheeks, he started a heavy attack on the other's midrift. Once, twice he landed. Gauging the distance as best he could in the darkness, Dan cut loose with a wicked blow. It landed hard and jolting under his assailant's heart and he heard a sharp cry of pain. The man staggered toward the other side of the platform and Dan leaped after him.

Dan tried to stop but it was too late. An arm swished through the air and a blackjack thudded against Dan's head. The press agent went down in a heap, all the fight gone out of him. He was out, cold, for at least a minute. The unknown bent over him, patting Dan's pockets for a gun. Finding none, he stepped to the railing and looked ahead. Returning to

the platform he struggled with the limp body
of the press agent.

Later it all seemed like a nightmare to Dan.
He could recall being dragged along the floor
of the vestibule, but he was powerless to move
his own muscles. It must have been a painfully
slow process, that task of lifting Dan's body up
on the railing and holding it there, but the assailant finally accomplished it.

The train rumbled onto a trestle and the
deep-toned thunder of its passing aroused Dan's
deadened senses. The cold night air cut
through his befogged brain and in a flash he
realized that he was about to be pitched from
the train. Rallying his strength, he clutched
desperately at his attacker. Already he was
falling. Dan grabbed at the railing and managed to hang on. His feet dangled almost to
the timbers of the trestle. He swung them
onto the lower step and prepared to climb back
to the vestibule. Looking up he saw the
other man bending down, the blackjack in his
hands. Dan tried desperately to distinguish
the features of the man above him but the night
was too heavy. The blackjack came down
sharply and Dan's right hand went numb.

Now only his left hand clung to the railing. Again the blackjack descended.

The train was still rumbling over the trestle and Dan, twisting, caught the blackness of water below. It would be better to land in the water than to be hurled onto the bridge timbers, perhaps knocked senseless by the shock, and then topple into the water.

With a mighty kick of his legs against the lower step, he hurled himself clear of the trestle and plunged downward. Dan steeled himself for the shock. He managed to turn and went into the water feet first. He went under, came up gasping, and found that he could just touch bottom. He had apparently fallen into the backwater of some stream. Moving slowly, Dan made his way toward the end of the trestle. He crawled out on the bank and climbed up to the right-of-way. Far down the rails the red lights of the circus train were vanishing around a curve.

Dan was chilled through and almost exhausted from his fight on the back platform. Every bone in his body ached and he was trembling from his water-soaked clothing and the chill air. There was no sign of a nearby farmhouse and Dan started trudging down the right-of-way. Flailing his arms to keep the blood racing through his body, he stumbled over the ties and crushed rock ballast. He had walked for perhaps fifteen minutes when an engine whistle sounded behind him. There was a glow of light as a train came into view.

Dan stood between the rails, waving his arms over his head as the train approached. The engineer whistled a sharp warning but Dan refused to move. The exhaust slowed and he heard the brakes go on. The engine came to a stop less than 50 feet away and an angry engineer stuck his head out the window.

"What's the idea of stopping this fast freight?" he demanded.

"Say, you can't get aboard this engine," he added as Dan started to climb up the steps into the cab.

"I'm the press agent for the Great United," explained Dan. "Our train is just ahead. Someone threw me off the back end while we were going over the trestle back there. I was so cold and wet I had to stop the first train along."

Dan stepped close to the boiler, grateful for the warmth of the cab.

The engineer looked him over suspiciously.

"You say someone threw you off the train?"

"Do you think I jumped into the water just for fun?" replied Dan. Reaching into the inner pocket of his coat he produced his leather billfold and from the water-soaked folder brought out his credential card.

The engineer looked at it under the shaded light in the cab.

"It looks all right," he said. "Anyway, we can't waste any more time out here on the road. Get over with the fireman and we'll carry you into the division at Waverly. I guess your outfit plays there tomorrow."

Dan thanked the engineer and the fireman made room for him on the left side. The engineer dropped his reserve lever ahead, released the air, cracked the throttle, and they lumbered away.

The fireman dug into his locker and brought out a coat.

"Better put this on," he said.

Dan threw the coat over his shoulders and while the fast freight roared through the night, he sat beside the boiler until his clothing steamed dry.

It was nearly an hour later when they passed the circus train, which had been put on a siding to allow the passage of the fast freight.

"There's your outfit," cried the engineer as they roared by. "We'll be in Waverly an hour ahead of them."

It was daylight when the freight snaked its way through the maze of sidings that marked the division.

"I've got to report this to the trainmaster," said the engineer. He took Dan to the office where the press agent repeated his story.

"It sounds mighty queer but your credentials are in order," said the official. "We'll check your story when the special arrives."

Dan pulled his book of passes, still damp, from his pocket, and made out the necessary number to take care of the trainmaster, the engineer and the fireman and their families.

Then he went into the station restaurant and consumed a large quantity of hot coffee with bacon and eggs. By the time he had finished his meal, the red train of the Great United was rolling into the yards. The trainmaster met Dan on the platform and they walked down to the business car. The first man they saw was the general manager.

"Dan!" he cried. "We've been hunting all over the train for you. Where under the sun have you been?"

Before Dan could recount his adventures, Bob had piled out of his berth, thrown a bath-robe over his pajamas, and joined them. Guy Chappell, the ringmaster, and Goodwin, who had also aided in the search for Dan, joined them.

"I was standing on the back platform," Dan explained. "I suddenly had a hunch some-one was behind me and turned just in time to catch a blow on the chin. I went down and after that it was a free for all. I would have gotten the best of it if this other fellow hadn't pulled a blackjack and slugged me into un-consciousness. When I came to, he had me al-most over the railing. I managed to grab on but he slammed the blackjack over my fingers. We were running over a trestle but I managed to hurl myself clear of the timbers and fell into the water."

"It's a wonder you weren't killed," exclaimed Bob. "How did you get out of the water?"

"It was only about five and a half feet deep and I waded out. I got back on the right-of-way just in time to see the lights of the train disappear. There didn't appear to be a farmhouse within miles so I started down the track. When a fast freight came along and I rode into town. We passed you on a siding outside town."

"Do you have any idea who threw you off the train?" asked the general manager. The lines about his mouth were thin and hard.

"Not the slightest. It was too dark to see his face. He was smaller than I am but he fought like a wildcat."

"Do you think you landed any blows on his face?" asked Bob hopefully.

"Hardly, I was working on his midrift. I'd have had the best of him, too, if he hadn't slugged me over the head."

Satisfied that Dan's story was true, the railroad official departed. Dan, accompanied by the general manager and Bob, went to his stateroom. While he was changing into fresh clothes, they discussed the mysterious attack of the night before.

"What was in the sealed package you gave me yesterday?" asked the general manager.

"I think knowledge of the supposed contents of that package caused the attack," said Dan.

"What do you mean by supposed?"

Dan stepped to the door and then walked up and down the aisle to make sure that the car was deserted.

"Just stand in the door, will you, Bob, and let me know if anyone comes near enough to hear us?"

Dan related how they had discovered the tampering with Bob's automatic and that the photographs had revealed fingerprints other than those of the owner of the gun.

"While I was sealing the photographs in a package," explained Dan, "someone watched through the keyhole. When I was convinced that I had been spied upon I returned to the city, purchased a duplicate folder, placed several sheets of cardboard inside and made it up to appear identical with the real one. I gave you the dummy folder last night in the dining tent and made no secret of it. I intended that whoever spied on me should know that the evidence found on Bob's gun had been turned over to you for safekeeping."

"Then why the attack on you?"

"The only explanation is that the man heading Barney Hutchinson's agents in our show fears that I know too much.   After the attempt to kill me last night I'll have to be on my guard every minute."

"Where have you placed the original folder?" the general manager asked.

"It's in the bottom drawer of my desk with a lot of publicity mats," replied Dan in a voice so low it was almost a whisper.

"No one would ever look for it there," agreed the general manager.   "It seems we're carrying more dynamite than I had expected. After this you carry a gun and if anyone else smacks you over the head, don't hesitate to use your weapon."

Chapter XII

CIRCUS WAR

Dan went to his stateroom where Bob dug into a bag of guns and produced a revolver.

"I don't need a gun," protested Dan. "The next time I'll watch out for a blackjack. I can take care of myself with my fists."

"The next time they may not use a blackjack," said Bob significantly as he twirled the cylinder of the gun, shoving cartridges into the chamber. He put five blunt-nosed .38's into the gun, leaving the firing pin resting on an empty chamber.

"Put this in your pocket," went on the animal trainer. "It's a well balanced gun. All you have to do is point it at your target and pull the trigger. You won't miss."

Despite the harrowing experience of the night, Dan had duties to perform. After breakfast, he went uptown to visit the newspaper office, provided the last-day stories and took care of the needs of the staff in the way of passes.

When he returned to the lot disturbing news had arrived. The Amalgamated was jumping the Great United's dates, slipping into towns and showing just a day ahead of the latter outfit. Fred, working with the No. 2 advance car had sent back word of the latest attempt to injure the business of the Great United.

Bob was intensely excited.

"It's certainly a dirty trick," he said. "The Amalgamated is about two days ahead of us and are cleaning up all along our route."

"What will Mr. Adams do?" asked Dan.

"That's hard to say. He won't take it without a fight. He's conferring with the ringmaster and the trainmaster in the ticket wagon right now. It will be something out of the ordinary, you can bet on that."

When the conference in the ticket wagon ended half an hour later, Bill Duffy hurried away in the direction of the railroad yards. The general manager came out of the wagon but he gave no sign that he intended to divulge the results of the conference and Guy Chappell was likewise silent.

The lot buzzed with speculation all afternoon on what the Great United would do to meet the latest attack. When Dan returned to the railroad yards he found a switch engine busy realigning the cars in the train. It was being divided into two compact sections, one of 18 cars and the other of 20. The animal cars, flats for the cook tent and equipment, the menagerie and the smaller tents and the pullmans were in the longer section.

Just before the night performance started, word was sent around that all of the performers were to be aboard their cars before 11 o'clock. An early departure was scheduled.

There was a large crowd on hand for the evening show and Dan watched the performance from start to finish. It was something that would never grow old. Each day it was a little different. Some clown pulled a new stunt, the tumblers had devised an extra twist or turn to add to their routine, or the aërialists were more daring than usual.

When the big show was over, the roustabouts swung into action with the precision of a great machine. There was no lost time, no waste motion. Performers hurried to get off their makeup and into street clothes. Well before 11 o'clock everyone was aboard the train.

Bill Duffy ran alongside making sure that everything was ready. The general manager hurried into the business car and called Dan into his office.

"We're going to skip our next town, Oxford," he explained, "and jump to Beaumont where the Amalgamated is trying to steal our date tomorrow. This section will stop at Oxford for water. I want you to get off there, see the editor of the paper in the morning, pay him in full for the advertisements we have run, and give him a complete explanation of the reason why we missed his town. Also inform him that we hope to return later and fill our engagement but that the cut-throat tactics of the Amalgamated compels us to fight back at them in their own way."

The engine whistled a highball, cries of "all aboard" sounded along the train, and the first section jerked into motion. The general manager, who was to ride the second train dropped off on the station platform.

Bob, who had swung onto one of the head pullmans, came back into the car.

"The war begins in earnest tomorrow," he said as the train rapidly picked up speed.

"We'll have to be on our guard more than ever. We played a lot of 'same day dates' with the Amalgamated last season and they make it tough every minute they're in town. Our huskies are fairly itching to grab tent stakes and pile into them but Mr. Adams won't stand for it."

Yard lights flashed by and the trucks clacked over the rail joints at a faster pace.

"With this 200 mile jump ahead of us," said Dan, "we're running almost on fast passenger time."

"I'm going to roll in," said Bob. "Better come along."

"There isn't going to be much sleep for me tonight. I've got to get at Oxford and explain why we're jumping the town to the editor of the paper there. If I go to sleep I'm sure to miss the stop."

Bob went to the stateroom and Dan turned down the lights in the office and pulled a chair up to the full length windows at the rear of the car. There was no moon but the night was clear. He relaxed and watched the special whirl through sleeping villages.

It was 2:10 when the first section ground to

a stop in the yards at Oxford.   Dan dropped off the back end.   He watched the train pull out and then went into the station to inquire about the second section.

"It's only 40 minutes behind," replied the operator.   "It took water at Alburnett and won't stop here."

Dan decided to watch the second section through Oxford and he waited at the station. With a shriek of its whistle and glare of dazzling brilliance the hulking fast freight engine swept down the main line.

The ground trembled as the steel monster plunged through the night.   Dan caught the flare of the fire as the fireman baled more coal into the hungry maw and he saw Bill Duffy's head behind that of the engineer.   The trainmaster was riding the cab, determined to see that there was no time lost along the way.

The second section was a swaying crimson streak, thundering past the station.   Roustabouts who usually slept in the canvas wagons stared out from under them with white faces. The special was doing 50 miles an hour through the Oxford yards.   The red markers gleamed on the rear car.   Then there was only the smell of rotten smoke to tell of the passing of the train.

Dan went uptown to a hotel and went to bed after leaving word for the clerk to call him at 7:30 o'clock. After breakfast he went directly to the office of the Oxford Argus. The press agent explained in detail why the Great United had cancelled its date and he found the editor sympathetic. The newspaperman promised to run a complete story and Dan sat down at a typewriter and wrote nearly a column. He then went down to the business office of the paper and settled in full for the advertising which had appeared. After that he caught a limited and arrived in Beaumont just before the afternoon performance.

The first person Dan saw was Bill Duffy. The big Irish trainmaster was raging up and down the platform.

"What's the matter, Bill?"

The trainmaster looked at Dan through eyes red-rimmed from lack of sleep.

"Take a look at the yards," he said, waving his hand toward a jumble of red and orange cars. "How under the sun am I going to get our cars out of that mess?"

On every hand were the red cars of the Great United and the orange flats of the Amalgamated. It looked like a hopeless mess.

"The yardmaster here is either dumb or else in the pay of the Amalgamated," snorted Bill. "He started out this morning by shoving us on the wrong sidings with the result that although we were in first, the other outfit got the best unloading place and then took our lot, the best one in town. They're playing to almost a full tent while we've got a bare 1,500 out this afternoon. It won't be any better tonight."

There was nothing Dan could do to help Bill and he went on to the Great United's lot, which was located on the edge of the slum district of the city. The tents were crowded together and everyone on the lot was worried and out of sorts. The crowd was a bare handful in the big top but the performers worked hard to please them.

The evening show was a repetition of the afternoon performance. The crowd was thin while the Amalgamated, playing a half mile nearer the heart of the city, packed them in.

By the time loading started, Bill Duffy had his train switched together and spotted at a crossing where it could be loaded with little delay. So far there had been no clashes between the rival outfits but anything could happen before the night was over. The next town was Harcourt with both outfits playing there. It would be a race to see which could load and get away first. Bill was determined to get his train rolling out ahead of the Amalgamated and he had taken steps to make sure that the next time the Great United arrived in town first it would get the choice unloading spot.

"We're supposed to stay together," said Bob when the show was over, "Mr. Adams is afraid another attempt may be made to kidnap me."

Dan slipped his hand into the right pocket of his coat. The gun Bob had loaned him was there, ready for action when needed.

The yards were ablaze with acetylene torches as the rival crews raced to load their trains. The Great United was carrying eight more cars than the Amalgamated, but Bill Duffy's smooth direction kept the wagons rolling onto the train.

At 12:45 o'clock the Great United was ready to pull out while the Amalgamated, loading a quarter of a mile down the line, was still rolling wagons onto the train.

The engine hooked on, air tests were run, and warning cries sounded along the train. Two short blasts pierced the night. Dan and Bob climbed on the last car just as it got under way. They were still on the steps when the air went on hard and the train came to an abrupt stop.

Dan and Bob dropped on the cinders. Lanterns were flashing around the head end.

"That was an emergency stop," said Dan. "Something must have happened on the engine."

The general manager stuck his head out the door.

"What's up, boys?" he asked.

"Looks like something wrong on the engine," said Dan. "We're going up now."

"Let me know if it is anything that will delay us," said Mr. Adams.

Dan and Bob hurried along the train. When they reached the head end they found an angry group.

One glance was sufficient to reveal the cause of the emergency stop. The engine was on the ground.   It had been deliberately derailed.

Bill Duffy was in purple anger, so mad words fairly exploded from his lips.   He abused the engineer bitterly.

"I tell you someone slipped alongside the engine at the last minute and put that derail between the ponies and the drivers," explained the anxious engine-man. "Do you think I'd set my own buggy on the ground?"

"Engineers are crazy enough to do anything," complained Bill.

The division superintendent arrived breathless.   Bill explained the situation briefly.

"Get me another engine quick," he said. "Uncouple our train, jerk it down the line, and put new motive power ahead of us.   We loaded first and we're going to be the first out of town."

The division official looked helplessly at the derailed locomotive.

"We've only got one more engine here with steam up," he explained. "That's been assigned to the Amalgamated's special.   You'll have to wait until he can get jacks under this engine and put it back on the rails."

"You get me an engine within five minutes,"

stormed Bill, "or I'll file a complaint with the general manager of this road that will make you dizzy. Do I get an engine or don't I?"

"I'll see what I can do," promised the superintendent, hurrying away toward the roundhouse. The trainmaster followed hard on his heels.

Dan hastened back to inform the general manager of the trouble.

"It looks like another deliberate attempt by the Amalgamated to delay us," explained the press agent. "Bill Duffy's trying to get another engine at once."

A fast passenger rolled into the yards and ground to a stop a short distance away.

"We're not going to take any chances on losing our lot at Harcourt," said the general manager. He opened the safe, counted out a handful of bills and thrust them upon Dan.

Hurrying ahead, the general manager routed out a dozen husky roustabouts.

"Step lively, boys," he said. "You're going with Dan Tierney on the limited to Harcourt. Plant yourselves on our lot and hold it until we get there."

With Dan in the lead, the gang boarded the

passenger.   It was a brawny, hard-looking outfit, every man capable of taking care of himself in almost any kind of a scrap.

"Too bad we didn't have time to get some stakes," grumbled Bat Anson, the boss of the gang, as the limited rolled out of Beaumont.

Dan paid the fares for his outfit and then slumped down in his seat in the day coach to rest as much as possible.

When the gray dawn touched the circus lot at Harcourt, it revealed the Great United's advance crew in full possession and ready to fight any and all challengers.

Dan telephoned the chief of police, explained that the Great United had contracted and paid for the lot and was prepared to defend it against the rival show.   The chief promised to come down at once to act as a mediator in case of trouble.

The Amalgamated's train pulled in shortly after six o'clock and blocked the main crossing.   When it came to seizing the show lot, it was a different story.

Confident that they would have no trouble in jumping the Great United's lot, the crew of the Amalgamated started the wagons rolling off the train toward the lot. When the first wagons arrived Dan and his husky crew met them at the entrance to the grounds. The Amalgamated was unloading rapidly and more wagons piled down on them but Dan stood his ground and the chief of police backed him up.

It was then that Dan had his first encounter with Barney Hutchinson. The general manager of the Amalgamated was shouting mad at the costly delay.

"Out of the way," he cried when he reached the barred gate. "We've got to move our wagons."

"You'll move them all right," the police chief replied, "but not onto this lot. You're blocking this street."

"What's the idea," cried Hutchinson. "Trying to hold us up for a little cash?"

"That's about enough," replied the policeman. "The Great United has a contract for this lot and they have men here to hold it. Now get on your way or I'll slap a fine on every wagon you've got on the street and run you in for insulting an officer."

Hutchinson hesitated, debating whether he dared defy the law and rush Dan and his crew.

Just then the whistle of the Great United's train sounded in the yards and Hutchinson gave up any lingering thought he might have had about seizing the lot. After much shouting and effort, the teamsters got the heavy wagons turned around and headed for the more distant lot of the Amalgamated.

Mr. Adams arrived shortly afterward and Dan related what had occurred. The general manager was greatly pleased over the holding of the lot and he expressed his appreciation to the police chief.

The Great United had the edge over the Amalgamated that afternoon but with both shows playing the same town, it was impossible for either one to make expenses and the ledgers started going into the red. The Great United, carrying the larger show and train, operated on a daily budget of from $5,000 to $5,500, depending on the license fee required in the cities visited and the length of the train haul. The Amalgamated's budget was around $500 less.

Word from Jack Mathews and Fred Watkins on advance was not encouraging. The Amalgamated was billing every town with the Great United. It was a bitter, heartless battle and only a question of time until one of the shows would be forced off the road.

During the afternoon Bill Duffy alternately threatened and cajoled railroad officials until he had his train jockeyed around into the most favorable position for loading and by supper time the Great United was ready for a fast run to the next town.

At supper the "inner circle" at the executive's table discussed the circus war.

"I can't understand why the Langdon estate allows Hutchinson to continue his ruinous policy," said Guy Chappell.

"Most of the heirs are in Europe and the executors in New York have little knowledge of the show business or what has been going on. I have written to them on several occasions but their answers have been non-committal."

"You may get some action when Hutchinson's books go too deep into the red," said Bob hopefully.

"We may be drowned in red ink before then," replied the general manager a little grimly. "If it wasn't for Hutchinson's cutthroat competition we would be enjoying a most prosperous season but two shows can't play the same territory and survive."

"Let's get out of this section," suggested Bob.

"It might help for a few days but Hutchinson would switch his routing and catch up with us. We might as well stick to our original route and fight it out."

After the night performance, Dan and Bob stayed on the lot and watched the loading of the wagons. One after another they rolled away toward the train. The seats were packed one on top of another and the canvas of the big top was rolled into huge nets and lifted into the heavy canvas wagons. In a little more than an hour after the close of the concert, or "after show," the lot was bare with the last wagons rumbling away.

Kerosene flares marked the route from the lot to the train, guiding the drivers along the unfamiliar streets. Half way to the train the last five wagons were stopped at an intersection by a policeman swinging an electric torch.

"The bridge ahead's been weakened," he said. "You'll have to go a block to your right, cross the bridge over the creek there, and then come back."

The driver of the first wagon swung his team and the cavalcade rumbled away over the detour.

Bob and Dan, riding the last wagon, saw the officer standing under the streetlight and something in his appearance aroused Dan's suspicions. He dropped off the wagon and hurried toward the policeman. The officer, evidently apprehending Dan's suspicions, darted away and was lost in the night but his actions were sufficient for Dan.

"Bob," he shouted, "stop the wagons. It's a trick."

But even as his cry rang out, there was the crashing of bridge timbers, the startled shout of the driver, and the scream of sorely injured horses.

Chapter XIII

BEFORE THE STORM

Bob jumped off the last wagon and ran ahead with Dan. When they reached the wooden bridge which spanned a small stream a sickening sight greeted them.

The first wagon, a huge affair loaded with part of the canvas of the big top, had crashed through the bridge, pulling the eight horse team down with it. Two of the dappled grey beasts were motionless, the life crushed out of them by the big wagon. Others were struggling frantically to free themselves from the tangled harness and the mire of the creek bed.

"Where's the driver?" cried Dan.

There was an answering moan from the shadows beside the wrecked wagon. Leaping down into the shallow stream, Dan found the driver's legs pinned under the wagon. The man was barely able to keep his head above water.

The other drivers hurried up to lend a hand.

"Someone get down here and hold this fellow's head above water until we can get him free," called Dan. One of the teamsters jumped down and relieved him.

News of the mishap spread rapidly and a crew from the train, headed by the general manager, soon arrived. Behind them came one of the great trucks, laden with tackle to lift the wagon out of the creek bed.

The teamsters had cut four of the horses free and led them to safety beyond the wrecked bridge. Two were dead and two more were helpless with broken legs.

Mr. Adams made a quick survey of the situation.

"Give me your gun," he told Bob. Taking the automatic he quickly dispatched the suffering animals. Then he gave directions to free the driver caught under the wagon.

Shovels were pulled off the other wagons and a crew dug down into the creek bed until they could free the injured driver. An ambulance had been summoned and he was rushed away to a hospital for treatment.

The other wagons were turned around and

sent to the train over the route which had been originally marked out.

"Another dirty trick of Barney Hutchinson's," said the general manager grimly when Dan told how the fake policeman had instructed the drivers to make the detour. "Let's see what happened to these bridge timbers."

With flashlight in hand, the general manager and the press agent, examined the remains of the bridge. The light revealed the secret of the wreck. The timbers had been deliberately sawed just enough to collapse when a heavy load like a canvas wagon crossed.

"I'm going to get the city attorney here at once," said Mr. Adams. "This evidence will save us an expensive damage suit for the city would probably have sued us for a new bridge."

The crew with the truck was having a hard time righting the big canvas wagon. Several times they got it partially upright, only to have it slip back.

"Send for Maude and Bimbo," ordered the general manager. "They can get down in the creek and jerk that wagon unright. Then the truck can pull it out."

Within fifteen minutes the two elephants

padded out of the night, their work harness slung over their sturdy shoulders. Mac Herndon, the chief elephant man, was in charge.

Maude and Bimbo were old friends of trouble and they seemed to know what was wanted. Down into the shallow stream they plunged, old Maude sucking up the cool water in her trunk. Lines were rigged around the wagon and Maude and Bimbo lunged forward. Straining and tugging, the huge beasts pulled the wagon upright. Then the truck, on the bank, hooked on a steel cable. With Maude and Bimbo putting their heads against the back of the wagon and pushing, and the truck pulling on the head end, they finally got the wagon out of the stream.

The delay had taken an hour of precious time and when the wagon finally rolled onto the train, the Amalgamated was pulling out, bound for the next stop.

The two big shows dipped into Kentucky and then headed into West Virginia where a prosperous winter in the coal mines should mean good business for circus people.

After a month on the road, they were fighting each other almost every day, with both outfits losing money by the hundreds of dollars.

The Great United was first into Bellaire and as a result set its tents in the uptown show lot while the Amalgamated was forced to play down near the railroad yards.

It was late in May. The weather was warm and ideal for a circus day. Crowds started gathering on the Great United's lot during the noon hour and when the ticket office opened a steady stream of people pushed their money through the wicket.

"This looks like old times," smiled Bob as he observed the jostling crowd. "Maybe Stanley Godwin will be able to use blue ink on the ledger tonight instead of red."

The Great United played to a capacity audience that afternoon and just before the show started Dan walked down to the Amalgamated's lot. He bought a ticket and went inside. The menagerie could not compare with that carried by the Great United. There was only a score of elephants in the herd, the cat animals looked old and poorly cared for, and the wagons were all in need of paint.

Dan went into the big top. He estimated that there were not more than 1,500 for the afternoon show. The performance was smooth and well timed, but it lacked the sparkle and sensational acts which featured the daily routine of the Great United. The only high point of the show was the cannon act with the daredevil who performed the stunt being shot almost the length of the tent.

Dan bought a ticket for the after-show, which featured an Australian whip-cracking team and a half dozen trick riders. Even this was inferior to the entertainment of his own outfit, which starred "Boots" Burns, cowboy movie hero.

Dan took his time about leaving the show grounds. It was his first visit to the Great Amalgamated and he wanted to see everything possible. Strolling out of the menagerie, he paused at a soft drink stand to buy a bottle of pop. Less than 50 feet away was the white ticket wagon, which also served as the office on the lot. It was there that Barney Hutchinson made his headquarters. Dan had seen the general manager in the wagon when he bought his ticket but he knew that Hutchinson had not recognized him. The door of the ticket wagon opened and Dan stared at a familiar figure.

The man coming out of the wagon saw Dan and his face darkened with anger. Then he forced a smile and advanced toward the press agent.

"Hello, Dan," said Stanley Goodwin. "I'm surprised to see you down here."

"That goes for me, too," replied Dan. "I came down to see what kind of a show the Amalgamated puts on."

"Pretty fair, isn't it?"

"Not when you compare it with the Great United."

Goodwin realized that an explanation of his presence in the ticket office was necessary.

"I've known Barney Hutchinson for a number of years," he explained. "We were on the old Frank P. Hall shows. I thought perhaps a personal talk with him would bring about a better understanding between our outfits and might result in an end to this costly competition."

"What did he say?"

"He seems determined to carry on the fight and feels that there isn't room for two shows like the Great United and the Amalgamated. He's losing money heavily but of course he has the resources of the Langdon estate to draw upon."

"That may end some day."

"I doubt it.   They seem to have great faith in Hutchinson's ability as a showman.   By the way, I'd appreciate it if you don't say anything about my visit here to Mr. Adams.   He might not understand the good motives behind my conference with Hutchinson."

Dan agreed not to mention his meeting with Goodwin on the Amalgamated's lot and they returned uptown.

The air had turned oppressive and the slight breeze of early afternoon had vanished.

Bill Duffy was sniffing the air suspiciously.

"I don't like the smell of it," he told Dan just before they went into the dining tent.

"What's the matter?"

"I can smell wind," opined Bill, "and you can guess what a big wind will do to a circus tent."

During the supper hour there was not a breath of air stirring and when the meal was over Bill pointed to a thin edge of yellow clouds on the western horizon.

"I'm getting ready for a bad night.   There's

going to be wind and then rain. It's a good thing we've got a high lot or we might be all night getting back to the train."

Crews with sledges drove the stakes deeper, ropes were inspected to make sure they were well fastened and the Great United set itself for a bad night.

Dan had secured unusually favorable publicity in the Bellaire papers with the result that another large crowd was on hand for the evening performance.

The general manager was visibly concerned about the weather for a showman fears nothing more than a flow-down when the tent is crowded with people. Panic always ensues, women and children are trampled and the resulting damage suits can ruin a show.

Inside the big top the band was blaring loudly while in the west the bank of yellow clouds mounted higher. Bill Duffy, husky Irishman that he was, admitted that he was scared.

"We've got more than 5,000 people inside that tent," he said, "and the wind is going to rip things up in less than half an hour."

"I've never known you to fail on a prediction

of wind," the general manager told Bill. "We're having trouble enough with the Amalgamated without piling a lot of personal injury suits on top. I'm calling off the show. Run the ticket wagon out onto the street where they can get their money back without being in the road. We're tearing down at once. Get the animals back to the train immediately."

Orders flew to all parts of the lot. In the big top Guy Chappell announced that due to the threatening weather and the desire of the management to protect its patrons, the evening performance would not be given. Money would be refunded at the ticket office or could be obtained uptown the next day from an office which would be maintained there.

Before the crowd started out of the tents, the menagerie wagons were rolling toward the train. Even the elephants were pressed into service to speed the loading. The smaller tents came down with a rush. Then the menagerie top was struck.

The air was still heavy but slight puffs of wind billowed the canvas of the big top. From the west there was a distant rumble and lightning flicked the heavens.

The performers hurried toward the train and the roustabouts redoubled their efforts to get everything on the ground before the wind struck.

"Get that big top down, boys," shouted the general manager as a vicious blast of wind swept the grounds. The top of the tent surged upward and Dan saw sidepoles jerked off the ground swinging wildly. He could imagine the havoc those swinging timbers would cause in a tent filled with people.

Racing against the wind, the canvas crews got the tent down just before the main storm struck. With a howl of savage fury, the wind swept down on Bellaire. It raged over the circus lot, tugging vainly at the flattened canvas.

Large drops of rain pattered down. Then the heavens opened and a torrent descended, born on the driving blasts of the wind. Kerosene flares flickered wildly in the storm and men, garbed in slickers and storm hats, moved cautiously.

Wagons mired and Maude and Bimbo were called on to help the horses and the big trucks. The two elephants waded through the mud and water. They were used to this sort of thing and a bushel of carrots apiece awaited them when they finally went back to their cars.

"Wonder what's happened to the Amalgamated?" Bob shouted in a lull in the storm.

The Great United's lot was practically clear and there was nothing they could do to help.

"Let's go down and see," said Dan.

The lot down by the railroad yards was a scene of tragic confusion.

"Their big top's been blown to ribbons," cried Bob. "They must have tried to put on the show."

An ambulance clanged up off the lot, followed by a second and a third.

"That means there's been a number of injuries," said Dan. "Too bad they didn't have sense enough to stop the show and get people out."

"Barney Hutchinson would take almost any kind of a chance for an extra thousand dollars."

"How many hurt down here?" asked a man who hurried up out of the dark.

"Can't say," replied Bob. "We just arrived."

"I'm with the Bellaire Tribune," explained the newcomer. "We heard a man had been killed and half a dozen spectators injured when the big top went down. The Great United was smart and folded up before the storm struck."

They followed the reporter onto the lot and learned that the first reports had not been exaggerated. The wind had billowed the big top into the air, carrying with it many of the sidepoles which had swung like pendulums of death over the panic-stricken crowd. One man had been killed, and four women, two men and a child injured. All of them had been taken to Bellaire hospitals.

The lot was a wreck. The big top had been split wide open in half a dozen places. The menagerie tent was down in the mud and from beneath the sodden canvas came the frightened cries of the animals. Two of the elephants had broken away and were roaming through the city at large.

The ground was low and the rain had turned it into a morass. Wagons were bogged down on every side.

"It will take two days to get off this lot," said Bob. "This should be a lesson to Hutchinson."

Returning uptown, Dan telephoned the city editor of the Tribune and explained that the management of the Great United apologized for not holding the evening performance but felt that safety of its patrons must come first. From then on Bellaire would always be a good town for the Great United.

Before going to sleep, Dan pondered at length over meeting Goodwin on the Amalgamated's lot that afternoon. The treasurer's explanation had been smooth and plausible, but why had he been so anxious that Dan make no mention of it to the general manager?

Chapter XIV

MYSTERY OF THE ARENA

The blow-down of the Amalgamated at Bellaire brought an end to the competition for the next two weeks. The Amalgamated was unable to put on a show for three days and by that time the Great United was too far ahead to be readily overtaken.

The industrial towns of the east turned out good-sized crowds and the Great United's books were again showing a profit until the Amalgamated caught up with them in Pennsylvania. Heading westward again, the two big shows fought each other every mile of the way.

Ringling Brothers had played Pittsburgh only a week before the Great United went into western Pennsylvania so they skipped the great steel city and went north to Hagerstown, a thriving city which specialized in fine steel.

The Great United's was the first train in and as a result played the uptown lot, while the

Amalgamated was forced to pitch its tents far out on the outskirts of the city.

There had been no open clashes between the shows for the last week and Dan felt that it was about time for trouble to break out again. He confided his apprehension to Bob.

"I'm afraid you're right," agreed the animal trainer. "We're getting the best of the crowds and Hutchinson will take some means to injure our show."

That afternoon Dan watched Bob put his lions and tigers through their paces. Everything went smoothly until Bob faced Jup. The huge beast was in an unpleasant frame of mind and he lashed and roared at his trainer. Bob forced him on the perch twice and each time Jup came bounding off.

Dan watched him closely. There was something decidedly wrong. Jup was annoyed and he was venting his anger on Bob.

Just when Bob had Jup on his pedestal for the third time Brutus, a tawny, heavy-maned beast on the other side of the arena, leaped into action. With two of them rushing him, Bob was forced to retreat and step into the safety cage.

The crowd thundered its applause. To them it was all a part of the performance.

Dan saw Guy Chappell talking with Bob. It was evident that the ringmaster was worried. He tried to dissuade Bob from returning to the arena where Brutus and Jup were roaring their displeasure but Bob was determined to finish the act.

Seizing a freshly loaded whip and making sure that his gun was filled with blanks, he stepped back into the den of lions and tigers. Just then an excited attendant let the black panther slip down the runway. Always mean to handle, she saw her chance to get Bob and she leaped across the arena, a flash of screaming black. Bob ducked, crouching behind his chair. Jup leaped in from the right but a blast from the pistol discouraged him.

Brutus, however, was of a different stripe. The pistol failed to stop him and Dan closed his eyes for a moment. The crowd was silent, sensing now that Bob was fighting for his life.

Training, character, habits had been stripped from Brutus and the panther. They were back in the jungle, scenting human flesh and stalking their prey.

Brutus gathered himself for a leap. Dan saw that the ringmaster had picked up a rifle. He was on one knee, the gun trained on Brutus. If Bob went down Guy would finish Brutus at once.

Bob was playing the game coolly. Fencing with the chair, he kept both Brutus and the panther away. Then they both rushed together. Bob jammed the chair into Brutus' face and let the panther have two quick blanks in the face.

Scared by the smoke and flame, the black beast slunk away, the fight gone out of him. Jup had returned to his pedestal and with Brutus alone to handle, Bob soon forced the huge beast into his place. He stepped quickly into the safety cage as the crowd echoed its applause.

It had been a great show but Dan knew that more than once his friend's life had been in danger. When Bob hurried out, Maja Manning was the first to talk to him.

"You mustn't go on like that when Jup and Brutus start acting up," she warned him. "One of these days you'll slip and they'll be on top of you before anyone can stop them."

"I can't understand what was the matter

with them this afternoon," said Bob. "I'd get them back on their stools and they'd seem calm enough. Then something seemed to upset them and they'd start in all over again."

He went over to the head keeper of the cats.

"Have Brutus and Jup been acting queerly?" he asked.

"They were all right until they went into the arena," replied the cat man, "but they're trying to tear their cages down now."

Bob, accompanied by Dan and Maja, went down the long line of cages until they came to the double one which housed Brutus and Jup. The lions were pacing back and forth occasionally lashing at each other with their paws.

"Don't get too close," Bob warned Dan, who had stepped near the cage.

"Come here," said the press agent. "Look at those spots on their skins."

There were half a dozen welts along Brutus's back and almost as many on Jup.

"What could have made those? Did your whip strike them there?"

"The whip is only for noise. Wait a minute."

When Bob returned he had the head keeper in tow.

"What have you been doing to Brutus and Jup?" he asked, pointing at the welts on the backs of the lions.

"Not a thing and those marks weren't there when they went in the arena," asserted the head keeper firmly.

"I'd give a good deal to know how they got there," said Bob. "Something must have been stinging them but I didn't see a thing in the arena. No wonder they were out of sorts and ready to pick a fight at every chance."

"You'd better not work them tonight," advised Maja.

"Oh, they'll be all right. It wouldn't be an act without Brutus and Jup. They're the best pair I've got."

Dan had a theory of his own on how the welts might have been inflicted but it sounded almost too fantastic to voice. However, he went to the ringmaster and asked that he pass word around for everyone to be on the lookout for anything unusual when Bob went into the arena that night.

Dan's fine publicity in the Hagerstown

papers brought out a capacity crowd for the night show and General Manager Adams was in a jovial mood.

"Better sit with me in front center," he urged Dan. "With a crowd like this everyone does their best. Should be a great show to-night."

"Thanks, Mr. Adams, but I'm restless. I think I'll prowl around a little."

Dan made sure that the gun Bob had loaned him was ready for action. If his hunch proved correct he might have need of it before the night was over.

The press agent stopped at the ticket wagon where Stanley Goodwin was busy checking the day's receipts.

"Good day?" he asked.

"The best in weeks," replied the treasurer.

"Haven't heard anything from Hutchinson since your call, have you?"

The treasurer looked at Dan sharply and the press agent thought he saw a gleam of malice in the small, deep-set eyes.

"No, why do you ask?"

"I understand the Amalgamated has been losing heavily every day. I thought he might have changed his mind and gotten in touch with you."

"I haven't heard a word from Hutchinson since that day in Bellaire. I hope you didn't say anything to Mr. Adams about it."

"Not a word," said Dan.

The main show was on and the press agent prowled around the lot. Roustabouts nodded as he went by for in the parlance of the show Dan was known as a "good egg" and a "white guy." Even the lowliest roustabout realized that to Dan's fine publicity was due a good share of the show's patronage.

Dan met the trainmaster on the back lot.

"What's up?" asked Bill Duffy.

"Come along if you want to waste a little time."

"I've got enough to do."

Dan turned away but something in his determined air made Bill change his mind.

"Guess I'll trail along after all."

"You hear about the trouble in Bob's act this afternoon?"

"Yeah. Queer about them animals getting stung like that."

"I don't think they were stung."

"What's that?" asked Bill, stopping suddenly.

"I've got a hunch someone shot at them. A fellow could sneak in under the tent with a powerful air rifle and peck away at those big brutes until he drove them crazy."

"You're right," growled Bill. "I never thought of that."

"It may not happen tonight but if Bob was to be badly clawed and we had to cancel his act the drawing power of our show would be greatly curtailed and we need him worse than ever now."

"What do you want me to do?"

"Take the left side of the tent. You know all of our own boys. Move along there and nab anyone that looks suspicious. If they throw away anything like a stick be sure and grab it. We'll work around the tent and meet at the other end; then work back here if we've found nothing."

Dan moved cautiously alongside the wall of the big top. From the music he knew that inside they were setting up the arena. The next big act would be Bob's. In the menagerie Jup and Brutus were still giving voice to their anger.

The trainmaster met Dan at the front of the tent.

"Didn't see a stranger," he said.

"You may this time. Bob's act is just getting under way. Better take a club along."

Bill picked up a stake and started to retrace his route. They met on the back lot and Bill was commencing to lose faith in Dan's hunch.

"I'll make one more round," the trainmaster said.

Dan was halfway along the right side of the big top when he saw the canvas sidewall move slightly. It might have been caused by a man wriggling underneath.

Dan hurried forward. He raised the sidewall cautiously, halfway expecting to see a man crouched on the other side. There was no one there but he caught a glimpse of the arena and what he saw there was not a pleasant sight. Bob was in a tight spot. Brutus and Jup were on another rampage. Every time Bob worked them toward their pedestals and seemed to have them under control they would explode with a fresh burst of rage. Dan was convinced now that someone outside the arena was deliberately stirring up the tawny brutes. If it kept up much longer Bob might lose the upper hand and go down under a snarling, fighting mass of lions and tigers.

Whoever was causing the trouble must be inside the tent and Dan moved along under the tier of seats. It was light enough for him to see fairly well. No one was underneath. The band's platform was just to his right. It would be comparatively easy for someone to slip under there unseen.

Dan stepped behind the elevated platform. Bending down he could see the shadowy form of a man crouched at the front end.

"Come out of there," shouted Dan.

The man whirled and leveled a gun at Dan. There was no sound of gunfire but a lead pellet buried itself in Dan's left cheek. Mad with rage, the press agent hurled himself under the platform.

The gunman escaped Dan's first lunge and rolled away. Before Dan could regain his feet, the other was scrambling under the sidewall.

Dan got one look at the arena. Bob was down. Brutus and Jup were fighting over him. The great crowd was in a frenzy.

A red curtain of rage clouded Dan's mind.

He lunged after the man who had fled from the tent. In the uncertain light outside he saw the gunman in full flight. The wound in his cheek smarted but Dan gave the fleeing man a chance to surrender.

"Halt or I'll fire!" he cried.

The command was ignored and Dan pulled the revolver from his pocket.

Aiming low, he fired rapidly. Flame from the gun muzzle spat into the night but the report of the shots was lost in the pandemonium which filled the big top.

On the fourth shot Dan saw the man crumple and he ran forward. Before he reached the fallen man Bill Duffy joined him.

"Get your man?" he cried.

"Yes, but not until he'd started a riot in the arena. The last I saw of Bob he was down and Brutus and Jup were fighting over him."

"Then I hope you got this fellow right."

Roustabouts who had seen the shooting ran up with flares. Dan's victim was on the ground, his hands clutching his right leg.

"You've broken my leg," he cried.

"I ought to break your head," said Bill savagely.

Dan bent down and picked up a powerful air gun, the weapon which had been used to madden Brutus and Jup into the attempt to kill their trainer.

"This guy isn't badly hurt," said Bill after looking at the leg. "A couple of you fellows pick him up and bring him into the dressing room."

"I'm going back and see what's happened to Bob. I'll join you later," said Dan.

He ran back to the big top, where the crowd was still hysterical. Brutus was on the ground, dead, felled by one shot from the ringmaster's rifle. Dan hardly dared look for Bob. Then he saw his friend in the safety cage, his shirt ripped to ribbons and his hands clawed, but apparently not seriously injured. The general manager was standing nearby. It was apparent that Bob was determined to return and finish the act. Dan ran across the hippodrome track.

"See if you can stop the madman," said the general manager. "He wants to finish the act."

"I think it will be safe enough," replied Dan. "Jup will behave and so will the rest. I just found a fellow hidden under the bandstand who was shooting at them with a powerful air gun."

"No wonder they wouldn't behave," said Bob. "I'm going back. I won't have any trouble now."

"Did you get the fellow with the air gun?" asked the general manager.

"I had to put a hole in one leg to make him stop. He's over in the dressing tent now with Bill Duffy threatening to split his head open with a stake."

"Then I guess it's safe enough for you to finish the act," the general manager told Bob. "I'll step over and have a talk with this gunman. He cost us a mighty fine lion as well as almost getting our trainer clawed to pieces."

The man in the dressing room refused to talk. Dan summoned the county attorney and the general manager filed the necessary charges.

"I'll take your depositions now," said the county attorney, "and it may not be necessary for you to return and testify."

"We'll come back at any time," said the general manager. "I want to see that this man gets proper punishment."

Dan went to a doctor's office where he had

the lead pellet dug out of his cheek and the wound dressed.

Dan and Bob did not meet until they were on the train. The lion trainer had numerous patches of cotton and adhesive on his arms, but his injuries were all of a minor nature.

"I've got you to thank for saving my life," he told Dan. "If you hadn't ferreted that fellow out he'd have kept popping away until he had the whole gang down on me."

"How did you get out?"

"Guy Chappell had to shoot Brutus. That scared Jup and gave me a chance to escape. Another moment and the whole bunch would have been fighting and I wouldn't have had a chance."

"It's a good thing you made me take that gun," said Dan. "By the way. I need some more cartridges."

He handed the gun to Bob, who reloaded the chambers.

"I'm going to bed," said Bob as he handed the gun back to Dan. "After the trouble today I want a good night's sleep."

"I'll be along in an hour or two. I must write the story of the trouble tonight. I'm going to wire it to the editor of the Kearney

Morning Star. It ought to make a good feature and insure us of a big crowd there tomorrow."

Dan went down to his tiny office, rolled a telegraph blank in his machine, and typed out the story of the two attacks on Bob and the capture of the unknown gunman. In the story he featured the calm heroism of Bob. It was the kind of a story circus fans would enjoy. Before the train started he hurried to the station and dispatched the message.

Thanks to Bill Duffy's ability, the Great United was loaded and pulling out of the Hagerstown yards an hour ahead of the Amalgamated. The next morning would find them over the Ohio line, pulling into Kearney.

Before Dan dropped asleep, he thought over the events of the day. There was no question in his own mind but that the man with the air gun had been in the employ of the Amalgamated. It had been a desperate attempt to wreck the Great United's star act.

The clack of the trucks lulled Dan to sleep. It seemed as though he had just closed his eyes when a tremendous shock rocked the car. It was followed by a deafening explosion and Dan had visions of the Amalgamated's special plowing into the rear end of their own train.

Chapter XV

THE PARADE COMES BACK

The explosion brought Bob tumbling out of his berth.

"What's the matter?" he gasped. "Train wreck?"

"I don't know. Let's get out of here."

Dan threw open the door of the stateroom. The lights in the aisle had gone out and the car was in heavy darkness.

"No wreck," said Bob. "What do you smell?"

Dan sniffed the air. There was the heavy, penetrating odor of burned powder swirling down the aisle.

Doors of other staterooms were jerked open.

"Let's have some lights here," said the general manager.

Stanley Goodwin produced an electric torch, its thin beam cutting a swath through the heavy smoke which filled the car. The train was still pounding along the rails. Evidently no one in the forward cars had been disturbed.

"Looks like an attempt to wreck us that didn't succeed," said Bob.

"I don't think the explosion was under or beside the car," said Dan. "It was inside."

"Let me have your light," Mr. Adams told Goodwin.

The general manager hastened back to his office, Dan and Bob close behind him. There were no words necessary to explain what had happened in the office. The door of the safe had been blown open and contents of the steel vault scattered all over the car.

Goodwin bent down and checked over the receipts of the day.

"Whoever did this job wasn't after our money," he said. "Everything checks out."

Dan stepped to the back door. It was partially open and it appeared evident that whoever had cracked the safe had dropped off the back end.

New bulbs replaced the ones which had been shattered and they examined the full extent of the damage in the cold rays of the electric lights.

"Little of value seems to be missing," said

the general manager. "Wait a minute. I almost forgot the sealed package you gave me, Dan. That isn't here."

Dan could have guessed that the dummy package was missing after Goodwin announced that the money had not been taken. It was evident now that the Amalgamated's agent feared the fingerprints and would go to any lengths to obtain them.

They cleared up the office and set it as nearly in order as possible. The safe was damaged beyond repair and the door hung from one hinge.

"Better get back to bed," advised Mr. Adams. "I'll report this to the proper authorities in the morning."

Dan and Bob returned to their stateroom but it was a long time before they were able to sleep again.

"Haven't you got any idea who is behind all this trouble on the show?" asked Bob.

"I've got my own ideas, but you wouldn't believe me if I told you, much less Mr. Adams. When the time comes, I'll play my own hand," said Dan decisively.

"I hope it's a good one. This strain is fierce."

They arrived at Kearney well in advance of

the Amalgamated and even though they had the best lot, business was only fair. After leaving Kearney, the circuses swung through Ohio and Southern Indiana, crossed central Illinois and rolled across the Mississippi into Iowa.

Both shows were losing money heavily. It was simply impossible for them to get enough patronage in the same city and with their arrival in Iowa, General Manager Adams decided on a new plan.

Calling Dan into his office, he explained his ideas in detail.

"We junked the parade because it was too expensive to carry and took too much time to put it on," he said. "I happen to know that the Amalgamated doesn't have any parade wagons while I've got half a barn full of them. I'm wiring winter quarters this morning to get them out, rush them through the paint shop and ship them to us at Iowa City. We'll be in there next week after playing the river towns. I want you to arrange for the proper publicity. I'll have pictures of some of the big wagons taken while they're going through the paint shop and you can have cuts and mats made from them.   What do you think of the plan?"

"It certainly ought to draw the country people into town and once they're in they'll be likely to come down and see the show."

"That's my idea.   I believe putting the parade back into the routine will be our salvation. Tell Guy Chappell I want to see him."

The ringmaster and the general manager held a long conference on plans for the parade. The announcement was made that afternoon and most of the performers were glad enough to see the colorful spectacle put back on the show.

"Is this going to mean a lot more cars?" Dan asked the trainmaster.

"About four," replied Bill.   "It won't take a lot of parade equipment with the menagerie wagons we're carrying now."

During the week the Great United, with the Amalgamated at its heels, played the river towns, Dubuque, Clinton, Davenport, Muscatine and Burlington.   Then it headed into the heart of the tall corn state.

The cars with the parade wagons were to be picked up at Iowa City and when the special pulled in there Monday morning, four red flats carrying the additional equipment were on a siding.

For the first time in several weeks the Amalgamated had skipped the date, playing in Cedar Rapids, 30 miles north. It would be back fighting again when the circus pulled into Des Moines two days later.

The lot was only three blocks from the crossing where the train unloaded and the wagons almost rolled down the grade of their own accord. The grounds were large and level, with plenty of shade, and the task of setting up the tent city went ahead at a fast pace.

After breakfast Dan returned to the yards where a crew was busy getting the new equipment unloaded. The parade was to depict a pageant of the nations with each wagon representing a different country. The wagons were gorgeously painted in bright hues and would make a colorful spectacle. Even the old calliope had been brought from winter quarters.

The wagons were rolled down to the lot for the assembly of the parade equipment and Dan went uptown to call at the Press-Citizen office, the town's afternoon newspaper. The Great United had received unusually favorably publicity and he found the city editor, Eddie Green, a live, energetic newspaperman.

"We'd like something different in the way of a day after story," explained the city editor. "Could you arrange to have our society editor and feature writer, Betty Baxter, appear in the parade or take part in the pageant?"

"I think it could be arranged," agreed Dan.

The society editor was a dark-haired, slight girl, who asked few questions but had an inherent newspaper ability to absorb everything that was going on.

When Dan returned to the lot he introduced her to the ringmaster and after making arrangements for her to ride in the parade and the pageant, turned her over to Maja, who gave the newspaperwoman a thorough insight into the life under the big tops.

The lot was alive with activity for with the parade going on at noon there could be no waste time.

The elephants were harnessed and the huge coverings of blue velvet flung over their backs. Girls in costume hurriedly took their places on the wagons. The band was split into three sections to make three small bands and a clown band tooted away with great discord. The calliope, oozing steam, broke into melody.

"I'm glad we've brought the parade back," said the general manager. "This is like old times."

The ringmaster hurried up.

"It's 11:45 o'clock. We'd better start."

"Give the signal," replied the general manager.

Dan found Bob near the gate for the animal trainer was not required to take part in the parade.

"I'm just kid enough to want to see this with the crowd uptown," cried Dan. "Here's a cab."

The taxi deposited them on a downtown corner. The business district was thronged with people awaiting the arrival of the parade. University of Iowa students, out of classes for the noon hour, paused to see the spectacle.

"Those students will make it tough if they don't like our show," said Bob. "A few years ago they almost wrecked a circus but if they like your performance they'll hardly let you get away."

"You won't need to worry," replied Dan.

Far down the tree-lined street the head of the parade appeared. Ten riders, in close formation, were carrying the massed colors of the nations. Behind them in a huge wagon decorated to represent the great strength of the British Empire was the first section of the band.

The parade was planned to cover more than half a mile, with the wagons and riders well spaced.

With the equipment fresh and shining, the costumes bright, and the horses stepping high, it was a spectacle of color and music that thrilled Dan through and through. The clowns cavorted along the wagons, some walking, some riding, and the clown police patrol in an old flivver chased up and down the street to the great delight of the youngsters.

The music of the bands faded and the calliope, at the end of the long parade, took up the refrain.

The last of the elephants lumbered by and the parade was over. Many of the spectators turned toward their homes; others who had come in from the country started for the show lot.

When Dan and Bob arrived the midway was

rapidly filling and the husky-throated barkers were commencing their cries. They found Maja and her guest from the newspaper at the executive's table.

"How did you like the parade?" asked Dan.

"It was thrilling," replied the society editor. "I rode beside Maja and was dressed in an English riding costume."

"I saw you," replied Dan. "You looked like a regular trooper. Be sure to give us a good writeup in the story tomorrow."

"I'll write columns if the city editor will print it."

The attendance at the afternoon performance seemed to merit the return of the parade and for the first time in weeks they had the crowd on the straw. It was a responsive, appreciative audience and the performers did their best to send them home tingling with thrills and the glamour of the big top.

Dan was standing near the ticket wagon after the show when Fred Watkins suddenly appeared.

"What under the sun are you doing here?" demanded the chief press agent. "I thought you were on No. 2 advance."

"I was until this morning," replied Fred, who looked dusty and tired. "Let's get some place where we can talk without being disturbed or overheard."

"Then we'd better go to my stateroom," said Dan.

There was apparently no one in the business car, but Dan shut the door. Fred peeled off his coat, bathed his face and hands, and then stretched out on Dan's berth.

"I feel ready for trouble ahead," he said.

"What have you learned?"

"Not a whole lot, but enough to know that the big attempt to destroy the Great United is going to take place mighty soon."

"Where did you learn that?"

"The boss of their No. 2 crew talked too much this morning. He had just received orders to bill doubly hard for his own show and to be ready to come back and cover up all of our own paper. He didn't openly say so, but I gathered that the cards were stacked so we wouldn't be on the road much longer. I thought I'd better get back here and see what you knew."

"I'm still pretty much in the dark," replied

Dan, "but I've got a hunch I know who is directing the attacks in our own organization. He is so prominently connected with the show I haven't dared take my suspicions to the general manager."

"Well you'd better get busy," warned Fred, "or we may be press agents without a circus."

The room was close and Dan opened the door. He heard a movement down the hall. Stanley Goodwin was coming out of his own stateroom, a traveling bag in his hand.

Dan drew back quickly and motioned Fred to silence. The treasurer hurried out the rear entrance, stepped across the yards and started uptown.

"There goes the man I've been suspecting," said Dan. "He doesn't know you well enough to suspect you're trailing him. Find out where he's going."

Chapter XVI

ON THE RIGHT TRAIL

When Fred returned twenty minutes later he was bursting with information.

"I trailed Goodwin to the interurban station and crowded up close behind him. He bought a ticket for Cedar Rapids and got on a car that was just leaving."

"Then my suspicions have been right," said Dan. "Goodwin is pulling out and joining Hutchinson. He's going to be in the clear when they make their big attempt to put the Great United out of business."

"What are they going to do?"

"I haven't the least idea. They may try to wreck our train. We've got to get to Cedar Rapids and see what we can learn out at the Amalgamated's lot."

The general manager had not returned to his office and there was no time to lose in hunting him up on the lot. They hurried uptown and Dan chartered a taxi for the 30 mile dash.

On the way to Cedar Rapids Dan related the various events that had made him suspicious of Goodwin beginning with the kidnaping of Bob, the threatening note, the spying through the keyhole of his door, the visit to the Amalgamated's lot in Bellaire, and finally the blowing up of the safe in the attempt to get the sealed package with the tell-tale fingerprints.

"Goodwin must have been worried sick when he opened that sealed envelope and found that it contained only sheets of plain cardboard. I'd like to have seen his face," smiled Dan. They reached Cedar Rapids well in advance of the interurban.

"You'll have to trail Goodwin," said Dan. "He'd spot me in a minute. I'll go out to the lot and look around. We'll meet at the union station around seven o'clock."

The Amalgamated had set up in the northwest part of the city along the Milwaukee tracks for they were to play the next day at Ottumwa and the Milwaukee was to transport the train that night. The equipment looked shabbier than ever but Dan learned that the show had played to a fair afternoon attendance.

Men on the Amalgamated lot were not inclined to talk but he thought he detected a note of tension.

When Dan rejoined Fred at the union station he learned that the advance agent had little of actual value to impart.

"Goodwin went straight to the lot," said Fred, "and talked with Hutchinson for an hour."

"I didn't see them," said Dan.

"They were on the back lot. Hutchinson has a small tent there of his own. I couldn't get close enough to hear what was going on but when Goodwin came out I heard him promise to meet Hutchinson in his car before the night show starts."

The sky was overcast and the dusk was thickening rapidly.

"If Goodwin is going to meet him again we'd better get out to their train. We may be able to get close enough to pick up something."

Without stopping for supper, they returned to the Amalgamated's lot, now aglow with light. The train was on a siding three blocks away. The press agents of the Great United moved cautiously. The orange pullmans were at the far end of the train. Lights gleamed in the windows of the last car, which Dan knew was the business car. It was there they would find Goodwin and the general manager of the Amalgamated.

They stepped cautiously over the cinders until they were close under the car. Voices came to them faintly but not clear enough to distinguish what was being said. Once or twice Dan caught the words "Great United" and he decided on a bold move.

"I'm going into the car," he whispered to Fred. "Everyone but Goodwin and Hutchinson will be at the show and I'll be able to slip into an empty stateroom if I hear anyone coming.

Fred protested that it was too dangerous but Dan ignored him. He mounted the steps carefully. The door was open and he stepped inside. Fortunately the aisle was heavily carpeted and his shoes made no sound. From the far end came the glowing of light and voices. Dan moved closer. Now he was able to hear every word. They were planning the destruction of the Great United, planning to send the rival circus to its doom that night.

Chapter XVII

IMPRISONED

Dan listened, horror-stricken, at the devilish plan Hutchinson and the former treasurer of the Great United were outlining. It didn't seem possible that men could plot such a deed, much less appear determined to carry it to its conclusion.

"You're sure everything is set for tonight?" the general manager of the Amalgamated asked.

"There won't be a hitch," promised Goodwin. "I'll hire someone to drive me back to Iowa City. All I have to do is give the boys the final word and they'll see that the Great United never plays another date this season."

"There won't be anything to link us with it?" pressed Hutchinson.

"They won't have a shred of evidence. Everything incriminating will be burned up."

Goodwin's last words gave Dan the clue he needed. They were going to attempt to set the

Great United afire, either on the lot or on the train.

The thing now was to get back to Iowa City and warn Mr. Adams to guard against fire.

A sudden desire to sneeze gripped Dan. He pressed his finger against his upper lip but he couldn't stifle the sneeze. When he looked up, Goodwin was facing him and the lights in the aisle had been snapped on.

"Who's that?" Hutchinson demanded.

"Dan Tierney, the press agent. He's the fellow who's been causing me all the trouble," snarled Goodwin.

"Well, Tierney," he continued, "it's a nice night to call. You'd better plan on staying a while."

"No thanks. I think I'll be going." Dan tried to force a grin but it was a poor effort.

"You're not going any place," said Goodwin. "You've heard too much. This time when I shove you off the train you're going to stay put."

"So you're the fellow who bent a blackjack over my head and threw me off the train," said Dan. "I'll remember to pay you back with interest one of these days."

"You won't pay anyone back," said Goodwin. "You're going to stay right here in this car until we finish with the Great United and then we'll put you where you won't tell tales any more. Smart guy, you and your fingerprints."

"Smart enough to have you scared so you shook every time you thought of them," said Dan. "Oh, I'll admit you're clever Goodwin, hiring that gang to kidnap Bob, writing the threatening note, putting blanks in his gun, and trying to throw me off the train but you slipped when I caught you on the Amalgamated lot in Bellaire. Your story just didn't ring true. Then you overplayed your hand when you cracked the safe and took out the dummy package."

Goodwin's small eyes glinted at the mention of the package.

"You'd give a good deal to know where the prints are, wouldn't you?" persisted Dan. "Well they're safe and sound and if anything happens to me those fingerprints are going to make it tough for you."

"Quit arguing," broke in Hutchinson. "There's work to be done tonight. Get into that stateroom."

He motioned for Dan to enter a nearby room. He was about to comply when he saw Fred stealing up behind the general manager.

"Get in there," barked Goodwin, advancing menacingly.

His words were the signal for Dan and Fred to go into action. With both fists flying, Dan sailed into Goodwin and Fred took the general manager by surprise from the rear. The battle raged back and forth in the narrow asile. Fred found that Hutchinson was no weakling and from previous experience Dan knew that Goodwin would put up a fight.

It was bitter, give and take, and Dan fought a cautious battle. Goodwin was like a caged animal, kicking and clawing. Dan measured him for a final blow. He caught the former treasurer a lusty clout on the chin and Goodwin was out even before he hit the floor. Dan turned to help Fred, who was finding the general manager almost a match.

Dan's skill and power soon turned the tables, and Hutchinson, raising his hands, begged for mercy. Dan lowered his battered fists.

"You're going on a nice, long trip," said Dan. "We're heading for Iowa City as fast as we can get there."

"I'm not going out of this car," protested Hutchinson.

Dan raised his fists.

"I'll go, I'll go," promised the general manager.

There was a movement in the aisle behind and Dan turned quickly. Goodwin was struggling to his knees, one hand tugging at his coat pocket.

"He's got a gun!" cried Fred.

Dan lunged toward Goodwin, but the other man rolled away and Dan fell sprawling in the aisle. When he regained his feet Goodwin had his gun out, covering both of the Great United's press agents.

"You're not going any place," he said savagely. "Now get into that stateroom and we'll take care of you later."

Under the threatening muzzle of the gun, Dan and Fred were forced into the stateroom. Goodwin slammed the door and locked it from the outside. Then they heard him depart with the general manager.

"What a fine pair we are," said Dan bitterly. "Looks like there isn't much chance that we can wrench into their plans."

"Maybe we can get out of this room," said Fred hopefully.

They tried the windows, but they were jammed shut and too narrow to allow them to escape. From the air in the room it was evident that it had long been unoccupied.

Dan sat down to think things out. Fred had been right in hurrying back from advance and unless they got to Iowa City and warned Mr. Adams, morning might find the Great United only a charred tangle of canvas, wood and bent steel. No matter how the fire started, he was sure that the Amalgamated's agents would be clever enough to make their own escape.

There might be human lives lost; certainly many of the animals would perish. A fortune would vanish in the smoke and flames; half a thousand men and women would be thrown out of jobs. It was fiendish, incredible, yet he had heard it plotted with his own ears. Even now Goodwin was hurrying to carry out his mission, to issue final instructions to the men who were to apply the torch.

If the Great United burned, Dan knew that neither he nor Fred would live to see the dawn. Their evidence would be too damaging. It would be easy to drop them from a trestle or shove them down between the platforms of the train during the night.

Fred had been making a careful tour of their tiny quarters.

"There doesn't seem to be any way out," he said.

Dan's hand touched something hard in his coat pocket. It was the gun Bob had insisted he carry. What a fool he had been not to think of it before.

"Get ready to run," he warned Fred. "I'm going to shoot the lock off this door."

Dan placed the muzzle of the gun against the lock. He fired three shots in rapid succession, each of them tearing away a portion of the lock. The room was filled with the deafening reports and they choked on the smoke. Then the lock gave way and they plunged into the aisle.

Chapter XVIII

ADVENTURE AHEAD

"Get out the back end of the car," cried Dan. "If we have to separate, hurry to Iowa City and warn Mr. Adams that an attempt to burn the show is going to be made."

The young press agents for the Great United raced through the darkened car and dropped off the back end without being detected. Evidently there was no one in the car or the Pullmans ahead to hear Dan's shots.

They commandeered a taxi returning from the show ground and Dan made a deal with the driver to rush them to Iowa City.

"Step on it," he said. "Every minute counts."

Dan and Fred eased back on the cushions as the driver shot his car through the traffic. Then they were out of the business district, heading down the curving ribbon of concrete that linked the cities.

"It's a fiendish plot," said Fred. "I only hope

we can get to Iowa City in time to catch Goodwin before he reaches the lot and spreads the
word."

"He'll be traveling fast. We can hardly
hope to do that but we can warn the show and
be prepared for the first sign of trouble."

"When do you think they'll make the attempt?"

"Either just about the close of the show or
after the train gets in motion. Think what the
speed of the train would do to a fire. It would
fan the flames and spread them the length of the
train before it could be checked."

"I'm thinking about it all right," said Fred
grimly. "I'd like to get just one good sock at
Goodwin. He'd remember me for a long time."

"The first thing is to warn Mr. Adams.
We'll take care of Goodwin in good time."

In a little over half an hour after their escape
from the stateroom on the Amalgamated's
train, the taxi slowed to a stop before the entrance to the show lot in Iowa City.

The grounds were ablaze with light. From
the big top came the blare of the band. The
performance was well under way.

Dan paid the driver of the cab and the press

agents hurried toward the ticket wagon. The general manager was in charge. Goodwin was not in sight.

"Where did you disappear?" the general manager asked sharply.

"I've been to Cedar Rapids," replied Dan. "Where's Goodwin?"

"I haven't seen him since the afternoon show. That's why I'm in the wagon."

"Let me in the back end, quick."

Once inside the ticket wagon Dan rapidly recounted the events of the afternoon, Goodwin's flight to Cedar Rapids, his own discovery of the attempt to destroy the Great United, the fight in the car, their capture and subsequent escape and return to Iowa City.

The general manager looked grave, almost sorrowful.

"I'm sorry it's Goodwin," he said at last. "I trusted him fully. It is hard to think that he could have violated my faith."

"Don't you believe my story?" asked Dan.

"Yes, I believe you, but it seems incredible that Goodwin could have been the man behind all of the trouble. Why didn't you say something to me?"

"I didn't have definite proof. It's hard to convince you now that he is guilty. What would it have been if I had come to you with an unsubstantiated story?"

"I wouldn't have believed it. You followed the wisest course. Get Bill Duffy and the rest of the boys here as soon as you can. We'll get ready for trouble."

Dan passed the word around. Even Guy Chappell appeared, turning the duties of ringmaster over to an assistant. A tense group gathered in the ticket wagon.

"There's going to be a showdown tonight," explained the general manager. Briefly he related what Dan and Fred had learned.

"Arm the men you can absolutely trust," went on Mr. Adams. "Post plenty of guards on the grounds. I'll want a man on every car of the train tonight and Bill in the cab to give the engineer directions if they manage to set us on fire."

"I saw Goodwin sneaking off the lot not half an hour ago," rumbled Bill. "If I'd known what he was up to I'd have broken his neck."

"Take every possible precaution. We've got to save the show."

They scattered to their various posts. Men who could be trusted were given guns and everyone was warned to get a stake and keep it handy at all times. Men patrolled the outside of the big top and extra lights were placed to insure plenty of illumination for the tear-down. A special crew was picked out by Bill and sent to the yards to guard the train. Everywhere there was a suppressed air of tension.

The show came to an end. The crowd flocked out and the men on the lot and the crew guarding the train redoubled their vigilance. Dan, Fred and Bob were on the move every minute. Somewhere in the organization they knew there were men who would attempt to start the fire. They were determined to ferret them out if it was possible.

Wagons were loaded and rolled off the lot. The big top billowed to the ground. Seats were piled in the huge trucks and a few minutes later the last wagon went lumbering toward the train. There had been no attempt to fire the show while on the lot.

Midnight trains east and west brought the loading operations to a temporary halt. Then the yards were clear again and the wagons rolled along the flat cars. Each wagon was locked in place with unusual care and Bill picked out men to ride on the various cars.

The general manager hurried out of the darkness.

"Where are you going to ride?" he asked Dan.

"I'll be about 10 cars back of the engine. Fred and Bob will be with me. We'll be ready for any emergency."

"Good. I'll be riding farther back. I've told Bill to keep his eye on the train every minute. We're going to run on a slow schedule so we can stop at a short notice. If a fire starts, we'll cut the car out of the train. Better to lose one car of equipment instead of trying to run to the nearest town."

When the train was loaded, a thorough inspection was made. Every car was searched but there were no outsiders on the train. The engineer whistled out of town, and the long train jerked into motion, bound for Newton, 85 miles west.

Fred and Bob swung onto a flat car as it rolled by. Dan followed. They were ready for whatever adventure the night might have.

Chapter XIX

THE SHOW GOES ON

The train rolled over the high trestle above the Iowa river, labored up the grade on the west side of the valley, and then dropped down the other side with gathering speed.

The night air was warm and it was not uncomfortable riding on the flat car, which was loaded with parade equipment. They climbed on top of one of the wagons and from that height could see the entire length of the long train. The night was clear and with the moon peeping above the clouds it would soon be light enough to see the men riding the other cars. Up ahead the sky went crimson as the fireman opened the door of the firebox and tossed in more fuel.

Running under a speed limit, they rolled along at twenty miles an hour. A paved highway flanked the railroad for a mile, then swung away toward the hills.

The special went through Tiffin, seven miles

out.   So far there had been no sign of trouble
and Dan hoped that the thorough precautions
they had taken would scare off the men hired
by the Amalgamated.

Bob was pessimistic.

"They'll try to set us on fire," he declared.
"If they'd go as far as attempt to put me out of
the way by shooting at my lions and driving
them wild enough to claw me up, they won't
stop at such a thing as fire."

"I feel the same way," said Fred.   "They'll
try to carry out their plans."

With the train held to a restricted speed, it
was going to be a long run to Newton.   At Oxford they were put on a siding for a fast
eastbound train that roared through without
stopping The guards on the train got down
and walked around.

"This would be an ideal time for anyone to
slip aboard," said Bob.   "A fellow could hide
over by that elevator or the lumber yard.   The
shadows are dense there.   He'd never be seen
getting on."

"Then let's go down the train and inspect it
again," suggested Fred.

They had gone barely a car length when the

engineer whistled out and the train jerked into motion.   They got aboard the car they had been riding, each one watching the train intently.

There was a long, hard seven mile grade from Oxford to Homestead and the special labored up the hill with thundering exhaust. Just east of Homestead they reached the crest of the hill and the volleying of the exhaust slackened.   The train picked up speed for the easy drop down the other side of the hill to Marengo.

Homestead station, dark and silent, slid by. The cars swayed as the speed increased.   The fireman baled in more coal and in the glare from the firebox Dan could see Bill Duffy looking back along the train.

The press agent turned to look toward the rear of the train.   Four cars back he saw a flicker of light.   Fred and Bob saw it at the same instant.

There was a puff of flame and a sheet of fire whipped back.   The air brakes went on hard. Bill, up ahead, had seen the flames and warned the engineer.

With brakes screaming, the special ground to

a stop just west of Homestead. By the time Dan, Bob and Fred reached the car, it was burning rapidly.

Mac Herndon was struggling with a man he had chased into the ditch along the right-of-way.

"Give me a hand," bellowed Mac. "Here's the guy that started the fire."

Bob plunged down the embankment to aid the head elephant man, while Dan ran to the back end of the blazing car. Reaching between the cars, he broke the train lines and jerked the coupling just as Bill Duffy came back from the engine.

"All clear?" cried Bill.

"Go ahead."

Bill raised his lantern and the engineer pulled the blazing car away from the last half of the train. He stopped several hundred feet down the line to await further orders.

The general manager came up on the run.

"Which car did they get?" he asked.

"No. 33. It carries the horse tent and some of the walls for the menageries."

Mac Herndon and Bob struggled up the slope with the captive. He was thin, with furtive eyes.   Dan had seen him a number of times.

"I ain't going to talk," he shouted at them. "You can't make me."

"Take him back to my car and see that he doesn't get away," the general manager told Mac.

"We'd better get this burning car off the main line," he told Bill.

"The next siding is at South Amana.   We'll try to drag the car there.   If the fire threatens the cars on the head end we'll have to cut it off and let it burn out on the main line."

They hurried ahead for a closer inspection of the burning car.

It was evident that it had been soaked with oil.

"Wonder where Ossie Babbs has gone?" asked Bill.   "He was riding this car and I figured I could count on him."

"The fellow we caught might have knocked him off," suggested Bob.

"We'll never get this car to South Amana," said Bill.   "We might as well unhook it here."

He went around to the head end and broke the coupling.

"We'll pull ahead and wait for this car to

burn down," he said, signalling the engineer.
Dan swung up beside Bill. The first section
pulled away from the burning car and Dan
heard his companion let out a yell of surprise.

"That car's rolling down grade," shouted
Bill. "We've got to keep going."

On the steep down grade, the slight shock of
the uncoupling of the front end of the burning
car had been just enough to set it in motion.
As Dan watched it gathered speed and rolled
down the grade. Flaming embers and pieces
of canvas dropped from the car.

The engineer whistled impatiently and Bill
signalled him to keep on. In this manner they
dropped down the Homestead grade toward
South Amana, the train moving faster and
faster to keep ahead of the oncoming car.

There was a deeper sound as the train rolled
over a trestle. Below them a shaft of light
pierced the night.

"That's the Milwaukee below. Must be a
freight," shouted Bill.

Dan looked at the train below. It was the
Amalgamated's special, bound from Cedar
Rapids to Ottumwa.

"Bill," he cried, "see that flaming car. It

may set the Amalgamated's train on fire."

"Serve them right if it did," replied Bill.

The blazing flat car rolled onto the trestle. Pieces of canvas cascaded from it. By that time the engine of the Milwaukee train was around a curve and it was impossible for the engineer to see what was taking place. While the special thundered under the trestle, embers and canvas from the car above started a half dozen fires on the train.

Fanned by the speed of the train, they spread rapidly and when the special came into view a quarter of a mile away, the whole center section of the train was ablaze.

The engineer, aware now of the disaster which had befallen his train, was making a frantic effort to stop but he had been running fast for the grades ahead and the heavy train was slow in coming to a halt.

Bill and Dan dropped off their own train, which had slowed down, and ran across the fields toward the burning special. It was a scene of wild confusion. The animal cars were being cleared as rapidly as possible. The elephant herd, maddened by the flames and the smoke, charged across country, ripping up fences and smashing whatever came in its way.

A lion cage upset and with a savage roar, the huge beast leaped away to freedom.

There was no chance of saving the train, except for a half dozen cars on the front end and the pullmans at the rear. When Dan and Bill arrived, they came upon Barney Hutchinson and Stanley Goodwin standing together. There was nothing they could do to stop the flames.

Hutchinson looked old and tired. Goodwin was white. Bill tapped him on the shoulder.

"Don't try to get away. If you do I'll break your neck."

The former treasurer of the Great United nodded sullenly.

The livestock was rushed out of the animal cars in time to escape the flames, but the wagons, the tents, and the seats were already fuel for the hungry fire.

Mr. Adams arrived in a car he had hired at Homestead. He went directly to Hutchinson.

"I'm genuinely sorry this happened to your show," he said.

Hutchinson looked at him dully. Behind them the flames still roared.

"I'm through," he said.   "The Amalgamated's through.   You won."

"No, I didn't win," said Mr. Adams.   "You
dealt your own hand and you drew a joker.
It was only by the narrowest of margins that
this same fate did not befall our train."

"What are you going to do with Goodwin?"
asked Bill.

"Nothing.   He's disgraced.   No show would
give him a job."

"You're coming for a walk with me," Bill
told the former treasurer.   When he returned
several minutes later he was nursing a bruised
knuckle but there was a happy glow in his eyes.

The second section of the Great United was
brought down to South Amana and the train
coupled together.   The charred car was left
on the siding, and a wrecker from Cedar Rapids
came down to take care of the remains of the
Amalgamated's train.

At dawn the Great United whistled everyone
aboard and the train resumed its run to Newton.   They would be late getting in, but by fast
work they could hold the parade and put on the
afternoon performance on time.

There had been only one man injured during
the night, Ossie Babbs, who had been knocked

unconscious and dumped off the train while it was on the siding at Oxford.

"It's lucky only one car was set afire," said Dan. "From what Goodwin said when I overheard him talking with Hutchinson in Cedar Rapids, he had a lot of men planted on the show."

"He had about half a dozen," replied Bill, "but that little fellow was the only one with nerve enough to make the attempt. You'll notice we're short five other men when we get to Newton. The rest skipped out while we were delayed."

"Are you going to prosecute Hutchinson for the loss of car No. 33?" asked Bob.

"No," said Mr. Adams. "The Amalgamated is definitely through. Most of their railroad equipment is damaged beyond repair, they've lost their big top and all of their canvas, their animals are scattered all over this section of Iowa, and I've got a signed agreement from Hutchinson that he will never again enter the circus business."

"Then it looks like clear sailing the rest of the season," said Dan.

"We're going on to the biggest and best year we've ever had," smiled the general manager.

THE END